THE CLOCKWORK GAME

A TIME TRAVEL DETECTIVE MYSTERY

NATHAN VAN COOPS

Skylighter Press

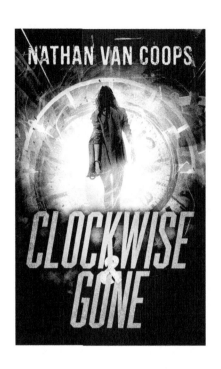

Get a free time travel novella when you join the newsletter for books by Nathan Van Coops. Get your free book here: https://BookHip.com/MGVVVFK

It is a truth universally acknowledged, that a time traveler in possession of a time traveling car, will be in want of a good mechanic.

That was my problem today anyway.

Jane Austen probably hadn't stumbled upon this particular truth, but it was just a matter of time.

I'd mention it if I ever ran into her.

I wiped my oily hands on a rag and tossed it aside.

The Boss was in rough shape.

My midnight-black Ford Mustang was parked in a horse stall, inside a stable that doubled as a garage. Owing to the demands of blending in across centuries, the Rose 'n Bridge Inn and Tavern had several such stalls. Two housed actual horses. They were starting to look useful.

I felt the weight of the part in my hands. It wouldn't be invented for another eighty years and without it, my car wasn't going anywhere.

I swore.

Another of the inn's animal residents stared at me from a patch of sunlight near the doorway. Clementine, a calico cat, seemed unmoved by my profanity.

"Know anyone around here who can retune a temporal ground analyzer?"

The cat's ears twitched and it gave me a slow blink, then it rolled on its side to stretch in the sun. Apparently it had no advice to offer.

I tapped my earpiece instead. "Hey, Waldo. Want to ship me a rare part from the future? Preferably without it costing our entire savings?"

"That is likely a job for one of your human associates," my AI replied. "I have no access to the time gate controls here. Perhaps Miss Archer can be of service."

Heavens Archer was the manager of this inn, and at that moment she stepped out the rear kitchen door, as though the mere mention of her name had summoned her. The screen door banged behind her as she descended the steps and walked toward me across the courtyard. I got the impression the sunlight got a little brighter too.

Heavens was taller than most women I knew but moved with the stylish grace of Myrna Loy. It was the common assertion that there wasn't a classier proprietress in the entirety of the time travel hospitality industry. I agreed.

Not to say she was perfect. As best I could tell, she'd never emitted a single shocking swear word, and she had once called baseball dull. It was an error in judgment I only forgave on account of her being Canadian.

Hard to hold a grudge against a Canadian.

Heavens walked up and offered me the packet in her right hand. "Hey, handsome. You've got mail."

Her word choice had my attention.

For the two weeks I'd been a resident of the inn, I'd been staying in a room across the hall from Heavens. Our relationship was strictly professional, but even professionals knew when each other looked good. Heavens looked like someone ought to be photographing her all day and then burning the photos at night for never living up to reality. Even today, in a faded rock T-shirt, jeans, and sandals, her attractiveness defied explanation. The closest I'd managed was that she was a woman who knew exactly what she wanted to look like every day and did that.

I took the package.

"Not heavy enough to be a car part," I said.

"You might have to press pause on that project."

I studied the return address on the package. The name said Rachel Rosen.

"Figured she wouldn't wait long." I set my temporal ground analyzer aside so I could better assess this new bit of mail.

The Rosen family had owned the Rose 'n Bridge ever since it had been converted from an old, English country inn to a time-traveling English country inn. From what I understood, it was among the least valuable of the family's holdings, but was an excellent source of revenue from wealthy time travelers hoping to vacation in exotic corners of the multiverse.

Just that morning we'd sent the latest band of tourists home after an excursion to 18th Century Norway. The inn had survived an authentic Viking revival festival with only minor smoke damage. That and a significant depletion of its alcohol reserves. The staff was now due for a whopping thirty-six hours of break before the next batch of tourists arrived.

"You getting away today?" I asked, turning the package over in my hands to view the seal. It was as good a stalling tactic as any.

"No. Staying in. You?"

"Figured you might be headed upstream. See someone special."

"Like who?"

"Rumor around the place is you have a boyfriend in the next century somewhere. No one seems to know his name though."

"You're a detective. You haven't looked into it?"

"I only snoop into ladies' private lives if someone pays me to."

"So noble."

I noticed she hadn't actually answered my question.

Heavens gestured toward the package in my hands. "Looks like you might have your next assignment. You think you'll make it back here after?"

"Hard to say."

I wasn't officially on staff but I'd been lingering at the Rose 'n Bridge since my last case. The beer was good, the food was better, and anytime Heavens was in the room, you'd be hard pressed to top the scenery. Plus, no one had asked me to pay my bill yet.

All good things come to an end.

Rachel Rosen's message was a summons.

I read the note on the back of the packet. "Huh. She wants me to call her before I open it."

"I set up the conference room for you," Heavens said. "I figured you'd want to talk there."

We walked inside and made our way down the hall, Heavens leading by a step.

"Whatever it is she wants you to do, remember it's optional," she said. "You don't owe me anything."

The fact that I was here at all and not sitting in a Time Crimes holding cell was thanks to Heavens. My last case had gone sideways with the law, and since she'd been the one to put up the collateral to help me make bail—a priceless original Michelangelo painting of herself—it was she who had the most to lose if I failed to satisfy Rachel Rosen. My case had been resolved and no one had a legal claim on me anymore, but Heavens and Rosen had been left holding the bag financially.

If I could free myself of that debt, I'd do it. The last thing I wanted was to saddle myself with an unspoken obligation.

Heavens opened the door to the conference room. "It's all set up for you. Just activate by voice control."

"Thanks."

I took a step into the room, but Heavens grasped my forearm. "Don't forget. Optional. I can always get another painting."

"Got it."

She released me and closed the door as I found my way inside. The room didn't look like a high tech conference space. It was an old study that smelled like pipe tobacco. It featured floor-to-ceiling bookshelves and four leather wing chairs. The fireplace was cold but the room still felt warm. There was no projector screen or TV. For touring purposes, all the future tech was well hidden.

I took a seat in one of the wing chairs and studied the package in my hands. My curiosity was piqued. I tore into the paper bubble envelope and extracted a small, framed photograph. One look at it was enough to make my blood boil.

I clenched a fist and barked at the room. "Call Rachel Rosen."

CHAPTER 2

Metaspace technology is oppressive. In an instant I was in another room. Not physically, but the cozy study was wholly consumed, holo-projectors disguising it with the spacious and no-doubt expensive office of Rachel Rosen.

The woman herself faced me, seated in an armchair, wearing a silk blouse and a serious expression. Her long black hair held strands of silver but her skin was flawless, making her look years younger than the six or so decades she was. The view out her windows showed the same olive orchard it had the last time I'd spoken to her, but now the trees were bare.

"Good day, Mister Travers. I trust you are well."

"Who the hell do you think you are?" I snarled. "There are rules to how this goes. Rules you should know."

She crossed her hands in her lap. "You opened the package."

I held up the frame in my fist. If she were really in the room I would have flung it at her. "I came to you in good faith, ready to listen. This is how you want to treat me?"

"It wasn't in my control. I received the photograph with specific instructions. I'm well aware of your hatred for paradoxes. It would not have been my choice in tactics."

I bit back my fury and glanced at the photograph again. It

was a black-and-white shot of me wearing a heavy wool coat, looking out at a featureless outdoor background I didn't recognize. A future me. "Where the hell is this supposed to be?"

"The photograph arrived in that frame via linear post. I don't know the photographer. But the correspondence I received with it insisted that you would be part of the current debacle I find myself in. The picture is proof."

I ground my teeth. "Did you know about this before Heavens came to you for help?"

"I did. The resolution of your last case was a foregone conclusion from my perspective. The collateral Ms. Archer provided merely added a convenient cover. Her kindness to you was notable, however. I can't say I would have risked the same, based on your reputation."

"But you're willing to hire me now."

"Forced, wouldn't you agree?"

"Photos can be faked."

"I had it checked. If there is trickery there, my best people couldn't spot it. You are welcome to inspect it yourself. But I find my options limited. As I suspect do you."

"What's the job? If I'm getting strong-armed into something, I at least want it straight."

Rosen took a breath. Sized me up. "The project is important, and while the method of ensuring your involvement might be distasteful, I can assure you that my goals are admirable."

"I'll be the judge of that."

She paused to take a sip from a teacup, then set it back on the end table beside her. "It's a historical recovery mission. I've commissioned a team to find a missing cache of artifacts from a Warsaw ghetto circa 1942. Are you familiar with the occupation in Warsaw then?"

"The Jews were all relocated to Nazi death camps."

"But not before mounting a resistance. Detailed documents

of the occupation were hidden, along with many treasures belonging to interned families. The items were divided up for safekeeping. Two caches were recovered in linear time. The team I commissioned was tasked with relocating the final cache to the future. It will be a priceless historical asset to the descendants of the families we lost."

"*Was* tasked? What went wrong?"

"I received notice that the artifacts were recovered and properly displaced per the assignment. However, the courier who was meant to bring the retrieval anchor never made the rendezvous."

"You hid the treasure in time? Jumped it forward?"

"It's the safest way to protect an asset across a century of marauders and hazardous conditions. But the time and location of the treasure's return was kept secret. Only the courier held the key to its arrival."

"That common?"

"When the courier is well trusted."

"Now you need someone to find them."

"The courier was carrying a specific item. The pendulum of a grandfather clock once owned by members of my family. The pendulum designates the time and location of the treasure's return. I would like you to discover what happened to the courier and recover that pendulum."

"Where was the rendezvous with the courier supposed to happen?"

"You'll find the coordinates for a time gate jump on the inside of the picture frame I sent you. It's a remote location managed by an associate of mine. His name is Winston Carlisle."

"What's your association with him?"

"Nothing personal, but we have been members of an exclusive club together for some time. The ACC. You might have heard of it."

"The Anti-Clockwise Club?" I shook my head. "Isn't being a time traveler exclusive enough company? You rich people are always drawing circles within circles."

"I'm sorry we can't all be working class enough to suit your world view. Wealth brings its own difficulties along with its privileges. Should I ever need a self-righteous assessment of my lifestyle, I'll know who to ask. For now, I'd prefer to keep to the task at hand."

"Fine. I find your courier, bring back your pendulum, then we're free of each other?"

"Suits me perfectly."

I tucked the framed photo back in the envelope it had come in. "What's the name of this courier?"

"Logan Tyler. Though I presume it may be an alias. These courier companies often keep the identities of their agents a secret for security purposes. You've been given a code card to identify you to the courier as my representative. It's in the package."

"Which relocation agency? You had to use someone you trusted."

"The relocation agent's name was Weintraub. A friend of Carlisle's. I only met him once but he impressed me. A dynamic and intelligent man. His manner and presentation engendered trust."

"You heard from him since?"

"No. And that is bothersome."

"Maybe your instincts are no good."

"I am trusting *you* with this, so perhaps you have a point."

I rose. "I'm going to use the time gate here at the inn. You can clear it with the temporal permitting department."

"I'll lump the permitting fees in with your sizable bar tab as an expense. I'm sure my accountant will be thrilled."

"When this is done, Heavens is in the clear too. You agree?"

"Consider all debts paid. When I'm holding the pendulum."

I moved to the door. "I'll be in touch."

Rosen disconnected and the room blinked back to its original state. It was like the whole conversation had been a dream. I walked out. There was work to do.

CHAPTER 3

"This isn't even a destination I recognize," Heavens said, studying the coordinates on the back of the photo. "We need a second opinion."

I was seated at my usual spot at the end of the bar, enjoying a beer and the scent of whatever Manuel was cooking in the kitchen. Smelled spicy. I fidgeted with the code card Rosen had sent. It was just a jumble of numbers and letters to me but would mean something to the courier. If I could find them.

"There's no way around it. I'm going," I said.

Heavens texted something on her phone. "I'm asking Sol where this is."

Solena Thompson was the inn's engineer. Owing to the fact that she was responsible for moving the entire tavern around in time, I had no doubt she was the smartest person on the premises. But she wasn't going to change my mind.

"I'm not going to create a paradox. If the photo shows me having gone there, I'm going."

"It's illegal. Rosen can't force you into an action with foreknowledge of the future."

"Might be the law, but I still can't fight her on it."

"Paradoxes are bad. I get it. But you could be walking into

anything here. Isn't death a worse option than potentially, *maybe,* duplicating yourself again?"

I declined to answer by way of sipping my beer.

"You never did tell me about the paradox that caused this version of you."

"And I don't intend to," I said. "Ask Grey One if you really want to pry into my past."

"I'm not going to do that," she said with a sigh. "You're the one I'm concerned about. Not him."

That did give me a warmer feeling toward her. Nosy or not, she always had class.

The side door to the tavern banged open and Solena came in like a gale force wind. She was short, black, and fiery. Like a spark plug. "What's this about you wanting to know if we could go to some godforsaken timespace?" She glared at Heavens, then at me. "This about him?" She pointed.

Heavens put down her phone. "I was just asking if you recognized that location. And if something went bad, could we get Grey out?"

"Get him out with what? The inn? If you think I can just plunk this place down anywhere we feel like and fetch your pet man project out of some nonsense, then you really don't know a thing about what I do."

"I know there are geographic limitations with our footprint, and leveling issues, but I'm just asking hypothetically."

"Hypothetically if he gets himself into the nonsense, and hypothetically you want me to take an entire building complex to an uncharted, off-Grid, slanted, uninhabited island in the middle of the goddamn Pacific Ocean? Yeah, we could go and we would probably get the inn fused into a mountain and fracture it in half on unstable ground and I'd lose my license and we'd both lose our jobs and never get the building out again. But sure. Hypothetically." She perched her hands on her hips.

"So, that's a no," Heavens said. "Glad we cleared it up." She gestured to me. "You've met Greyson, right?"

Sol addressed me. "You saw where those coordinates go, right? Island of Attu. Probably called that because Alaska sneezed it so far away that you can barely find it on a map. Did you know they actually had to bend the international date line just to fit it in a time zone with the rest of the Aleutian islands? So far west it shares a timezone with Hawaii. I looked that up when I was trying to figure out who ever heard of such a terrible place to want to go."

Manuel walked out of the kitchen with a plate of tacos that made my mouth water just looking at them. He was followed by Mollie, his dog. Manuel put the plate in front of Heavens. "Those are for you, mi cielo. Made them special how you like."

"Thanks Manny," Heavens said.

He looked to Sol. She shook her head. "I ate already."

He shrugged.

"I'll take some," I said.

Manny narrowed his eyes. "You can order yourself a pizza."

He was still mad at me for scoring the room across the hall from Heavens. Apparently the guys had all been counting on a shot at it when Buzzy Fingers the resident saxophone player died. Not my fault it was the only room open the day I showed up, but Manuel was as good at holding grudges as he was at cooking. He stomped back to the kitchen. I waved to Mollie the collie and her tail wagged a little as she turned to follow her master.

"I can set up the time gate to get you there," Heavens said, still managing to stay on topic. "But how on Earth do you know they have a way out for you?"

"I'll have my chronometer," I said. "I can get back the long way if I have to. I think the destination is in twenty-fifteen or something. It's not the dark ages."

"Just about," Sol muttered. But she was from the early

twenty-third century and everywhere we went seemed quaint to her.

Heavens took a bite of a taco, then slid the plate toward me.

God I loved her.

"What about someone to go with you? Someone to watch your back." She wasn't letting up yet.

"I'll have Waldo," I said through a mouthful of taco. My tastebuds immediately entered a transcendental state.

"No offense to him, but I was thinking of someone with a little more substance."

I chewed and washed it down with a swig of beer. "You're overthinking this. I go. I do the job. I come back. Maybe I bring Manuel an Alaska souvenir and he makes me dinner. Everyone wins."

Heavens crossed her arms. "I still don't like it."

"Look on the bright side," Sol said. "If he dies, we'll get his car."

"See?" I cocked an elbow toward Sol as I took another bite of taco. "She gets it."

By the time I'd finished lunch and grabbed my duffel bag from upstairs, Heavens had the time gate programmed in the control room. She still looked pensive.

"Don't worry. I know how to take care of myself." I patted the Stinger 1911 in the holster beneath my jacket.

She was still frowning. "Something feels wrong about this. Don't you ever get a gut feeling about something? Your intuition?"

"Sure."

She sighed and pierced me with her brilliant green eyes. "Just promise me that if you get in a situation where something doesn't feel right, you'll trust your gut and get out of there."

"I never knew you cared about my safety this much."

"That's not a promise, Grey."

"Fine. Trust my gut. Got it."

She held my gaze a second longer, then activated the time gate controls. She'd already entered the coordinates. The emitters on the edges of the framework began to glow, and multicolored light pulsed through the space between them. It made the air shimmer. After a few seconds it was a brilliant wall of color.

I hoisted my bag higher on my shoulder. "Back before you know it." But I didn't step through yet. I turned at the edge of the gate, reached out, and took Heavens' arm. "Hey. Thank you."

She'd been staring at the destination coordinates on the screen, but she rotated slowly to face me. She put one hand, then the other, on my chest. She looked up into my eyes. Her face was only inches from mine. Her body was close. Too close for a couple of people keeping things professional. But she wasn't moving away. Her lips suddenly felt magnetic. My pulse revved. I eased my face closer to hers. Her lips parted, but then she spoke.

"Don't die."

She shoved me.

I stumbled backward and went tumbling through time.

CHAPTER 4

Time gates are instant. That's why I had no time to recover my balance. That would be my excuse anyway as I landed squarely on my backside under the overcast sky of wherever I'd just arrived. The ground was lumpy and vaguely damp.

A woman's voice spoke. "That's some entrance. You always show up ass-first?"

I looked over my shoulder to find the speaker was a fifty-ish Caucasian woman with hair the color of a hay bale. She held a knobby walking stick and had a canvas satchel strung across her chest. Her clothes were well suited for hiking, as was her face. It had the lean, freckled look from decades spent outdoors.

"I'm Mary Hurst," she said. "You must be the one from Rosen."

I climbed slowly to my feet and picked up my bag. "Greyson Travers." She didn't offer a handshake, so I didn't either.

"Most of the others are already here. Up at the lodge."

"Others?"

"Didn't think you were the only one coming, did you?"

I didn't know what I thought, but I was interested. I scanned the hilly, grass-covered landscape. "This is Attu, huh? They never heard of trees?"

"We've got grass and hills and clay and sand, but if you want trees you've come to the wrong island."

I turned to have a look at the time gate. It wasn't fancy. The wave emitters were rigged to a frame no bigger than a standard house doorway and the whole thing was attached to a hoist so it could be lifted into the back of a pickup truck. It did have a sort of awning to protect it from rain, but it all looked temporary. The truck was there too. A rusty, battered survivor from the 1970s. Beyond the truck, the land sloped away down to a gray, desolate shoreline and bank of fog that obscured any hint of a horizon. The gate had powered down now.

"Why is this thing so far out?" I asked.

"Winston didn't want it close to the lodge. Thinks it's a hazard." She glanced at the gate. "Probably is."

"Winston Carlisle?"

"He's up at the lodge. I'd offer you a ride but the truck has to stay. We'll walk back. You pack a slicker?" Mary's jacket was perfect for inclement weather, but I had to admit mine wasn't. My boots would likely hold up all right, but my trousers were already damp from my landing and my jacket wouldn't be much use against rain.

"There are a few things up at the lodge that might suit you better than what you have on. Soggy walk since it rained earlier, but this weather isn't all that bad for Attu. We'll be fogged in soon, but it isn't supposed to come down hard again till tomorrow."

"You've been here before, I take it?"

"Sure. Been coming out for years. From before the Coast Guard abandoned the LORAN station and closed the airstrip. No one is out here permanently anymore, but we still maintain a dock."

"You came by boat?"

"Someone had to. You think all this sets itself up on its own?" She gestured to the time gate.

"Thought maybe you'd jump in some other way."

She shook her head. "I'm not one of y'all. I'm in the club enough to know how you get around, but I don't need to go bouncing through time. Straight line kind of life is fine by me."

She was a linear. That was interesting.

"You work for Carlisle?"

"Worked with him before," she said. "This time somebody named Weintraub paid for my trip out. Not too many boats come this way anymore so it had to be an expensive charter, but I try not to ask for figures. Impolite." She knocked a clump of mud off her boot with her stick. "Let's get going. You don't want to miss supper."

I adjusted my duffel bag over my shoulder and followed.

Mary Hurst kept a brisk pace and didn't spare time for conversation, except for a pause at the top of a particularly steep hill.

"Look down there. Sitting on that wreck. That's a white-tailed eagle." She hoisted a camera from her satchel and snapped a photo.

The old vehicle in question looked like it had rotted away a hundred years ago. I wasn't far off in my estimation, as Mary took time to explain. Apparently it was all left-overs from WWII. The bird just looked like a bird to me. Big though.

"Lots of old junk around here," I said.

"Whole island is littered with stuff they left after the invasion. Mostly ground transports and old trucks like that, but there's a few planes too. The P-38 carcass is that way, and there's a bomber. I forget the designation on that. B-24? That sound plausible?"

I shrugged.

"Yeah. I'm more into the birds myself. Saw two Eurasian

wigeons this morning. We get all kinds of Asian strays here. It's the main attraction."

I tried to look suitably impressed. So far I wasn't seeing much else to be excited about. The terrain was difficult, and other than the snow-capped mountain peaks and the smattering of rusty vehicles, the island didn't seem to have much to look at.

We finally sighted the lodge. Mary Hurst stopped short. I caught her checking her watch.

"I'm going to leave you to find your way on from here. Your room is on the far side of the library. Someone can show you. I've got another arrival to meet in a bit and I was hoping to get a few shots of that widgeon nest before the fog gets to us."

"Anyone I know?"

"The birds?"

"The next arrival at the gate."

"You'll meet everyone at dinner."

She turned on her heel and headed back the way we came.

"Thanks for the help," I said.

She put a hand up in a half-wave but never looked back.

I watched her work her way through the tall grass for a while before turning my attention to the lodge.

It was a wide wooden structure about two hundred yards away. Due to the slope, it rested partially on stilts and featured a wraparound porch along the upper story. Light shone through over two dozen floor-to-ceiling windows. Anything constructed on an island this remote had to cost a fortune, but this was over the top. The kind of place that only time travelers could get away with building.

I slipped my earpiece in and tapped it.

"Good afternoon, Greyson," Waldo said. "I see you've gotten us lost again."

"Tell me you have something for me," I said. "Any idea what we're walking into?"

"I can tell you that you are roughly eleven hundred miles from anything you might remotely consider civilization. Our communications are non-existent. Unless you discover a satellite-capable device, no one will be hearing from you anytime soon."

"Can you get us back to the time gate if things go badly?"

"Your Breadcrumbs app is running. I'll be able to map your movements, but I'm afraid you'll find my abilities severely limited here."

"At least you have your dauntless optimism," I said.

"There is one plus side to your location. If you meet an unfortunate end, there won't be many people who will ever know."

I shoved my hands in my pockets to keep them warm.

"Let's get on with it then. Mary mentioned dinner. That sounded promising."

I climbed the rest of the hillside, navigating my way to the southeast corner of the lodge. A weathered, wooden staircase ascended to this side of the porch and I climbed it. There was a faint sound of music coming from inside the lodge as well as several voices. A sturdy door held a brass door knocker in the shape of a toucan head. I knocked.

The door swung open, and the smiling woman on the other side of the threshold lost her smile. "Oh fuck. Nobody told me it was going to be you."

CHAPTER 5

The young woman in the doorway was Zhang Zi, a hacker and arms dealer who more commonly went by the name Zigzag. She wore a fitted button down shirt with suspenders and skinny-legged pants. Her collar was wide and her choppy black hair was styled in a pixie cut. She didn't look happy.

"Evening, Zig. I like the haircut."

She reluctantly opened the door the rest of the way. I'd run into her a few weeks ago in Shanghai, but that was in the future and I had no idea if she'd experienced it yet. One of the challenges of meeting other time travelers.

The space behind her glowed amber from the dozen Edison bulb fixtures that were mounted to the walls. It was a big drawing room with spacious couches for taking in the view. Faces looked my way. One was a stunner of a redhead in a curve-hugging dress. The other, a broad-chested black man in a herringbone vest and dark blazer. He rose from an armchair and made his way over. His smile was wide and easy. "You must be the agent for Rachel Rosen," he said. "I'm Winston Carlisle." He offered a handshake.

"Head of the club?" I took the offered hand. His grip was strong.

"Are you a member?" he asked. "Your face looks familiar."

"Just one of those faces."

"A good one," he said. "Welcome to Attu."

"Didn't know it was a party."

Winston smiled broader. "We have a great deal to celebrate."

The smoke show redhead approached. She was perhaps twenty-five and wearing a dress with a neckline that could make a runway model blush. Winston welcomed her to the conversation. "Let me introduce my colleague, Miss Ainsley Parker. Ainsley, this is Mister . . ."

"Travers," I said. "But call me Greyson."

The redhead smiled and offered a hand. Her eyes were bright. "'Colleague' is a generous term. Winston is the historian. I'm support staff at best."

"Nonsense. Miss Parker has been an invaluable asset to our club," Winston contended. "None of us would be here tonight without her."

"It's a pleasure, Miss Parker." I bowed slightly over her hand. "You all mind pointing me to somewhere I can unload? I was told I was staying near a library."

"How rude of me," Winston said. "Yes, please. Get settled. Miss Parker will show you the way. Can I fix you a drink for your return?" He gestured toward a bar along the edge of the room.

"Wouldn't say no to an old fashioned."

"It'll be waiting for you."

Ainsley Parker led me out of the room. I didn't mind the view. But I glanced back once and found Zigzag still watching me from near the door. She looked away quickly, but I couldn't help but notice the way her synthetic left hand was twitching. Nervous tick? I hoisted my bag over my shoulder again and followed Ainsley.

Two other drinks sat in rings of condensation on the table near one of the couches. Who did those belong to?

I figured I'd find out soon enough. This assignment was shaping up to be more social than I'd imagined.

Ainsley Parker led me down a carpeted hall and through the library. Looked like a lot of books on birds and WWII history but I spotted a few shelves of fiction classics too. Several well-stuffed armchairs were positioned around the room. There was even a fire going. If the party was a drag I'd have a fallback plan.

Ainsley opened a door in the far wall of the library. Beyond it was a spacious bedroom with a king bed, bureau, and plenty of walking around space.

"You should have everything you need," she said. "Ms. Hurst did a nice job getting everything set up. All the comforts of home. But if you are missing anything, let me know. I'll see what I can do."

"I'll be fine. You look too well-dressed to be running around worrying about me."

She glanced down at her outfit and brushed a hand along her hip. "It's a bit much, right? When Winston told me I was coming along, he said to dress up. I don't get a lot of excuses so I might have overdone it."

"It's a killer dress."

She flushed a little. "If you saw me on my normal day, you wouldn't even recognize me."

"What is it you do for Mr. Carlisle?"

"I'm an actuary for the club. Finance department." She watched me from beneath her long eyelashes. "Boring, right?"

"Winston seems to give you a lot of credit. Must be doing something right."

"He's just being kind. As are you, I'm sure. I'll leave you to unpack. It was nice meeting you, Mr. Travers."

"Greyson."

"Greyson," she repeated. She smiled demurely, then walked

away. She glanced back once near the door to the library and gave me a small wave before disappearing down the hall.

I let out a low whistle.

"Tell you what, Waldo. This case won't be dull with her around."

"Do you have an intention of hosting a *bedroom rodeo* with Miss Parker while you are here?" my AI replied.

I leaned my head back and rolled my eyes. "Not by that description. We really need to spend some time on your social vocabulary."

"I recently downloaded a thesaurus of sexual euphemisms I'm trying out. Would you like to hear more?"

"Most assuredly not. I'm going to quick-change and get back out there. We have a courier to meet."

I hadn't packed much in the way of dress clothes, but I managed a button down shirt and blazer over gray pants and my usual boots. Upscale utilitarian. It would have to do. I moved my gun to a clip holster on the back of my belt so my blazer wouldn't have a bulge. Nothing said 'party' like packing heat.

When I walked out to the main gathering area again, the two missing guests were back at the low table. I recognized both. One was a short, musclebound, white guy with a neolithic forehead. The distinguished, unfairly handsome black man to his right was the most powerful gangster I knew. His name was Roman Amadeus. He looked at me and frowned.

I was glad to be wearing my gun, because this party had just become a lot more dangerous.

CHAPTER 6

"I'd like to invite you all to join me in the dining room," Winston Carlisle said. "You'll find everything arranged."

The group in the drawing room rose and drifted toward the door he indicated. The aroma of garlic and herbs wafted in.

I tried to keep a wary distance from Roman Amadeus, but he intercepted me.

"Travers. Didn't know you had anything to do with this Rosen business. What a surprise."

"I get dragged into all kinds of trouble. What are you doing here?"

"You don't know? I'm a financier of this project. The club calls, I answer."

"Reputable people like the Rosens let you in their club? They must not do their research."

"I'm a businessman, Greyson. And a successful one. The members of the Anti-Clockwise Club recognize me as one of their own. Just like they recognize when someone *doesn't* fit in."

"Don't worry, you won't see an application from me anytime soon."

"That's where you're wrong. I believe the club has indeed

received your application, though it's the wiser, more successful version of you. The one we might actually consider."

My jaw clenched.

"Must be awful always being second best to a version of yourself who gets more from life than you. Just how *did* you blunder so badly as to become a duplicate? I don't think you've ever said."

I wanted to deck him. Then I'd kick him when he was down and throttle his bodyguard for good measure.

But Winston Carlisle chose that moment to arrive bearing my drink. The punching and throttling would have to wait.

"Old fashioned, as promised." He handed it to me. "I see you've met Mr. Amadeus and his associate, Mr. Leo DeRossi. They've been so kind as to supply us with the time gate for this meeting. In fact, Mr. Amadeus has been instrumental in funding for this entire lodge. One of our most generous members." His smile appeared genuine.

Amadeus beamed back at him. "Hard to think of a better use of my funds than preserving history, Winston. And you do a marvelous job managing it all."

Carlisle appeared to have no difficulty swallowing all the BS Amadeus was putting out. I wanted to gag.

"It's been a fascinating enterprise. Please come take your seats, gentlemen. Our guest of honor should be here soon." He bowed out of the way with a flourish.

I let Amadeus and his henchman have a few steps on me. I was in no hurry to have them at my back.

The dining room was spacious, with a table that could seat twenty. Only eight place settings were in use. The food was served buffet style and the others had already made their way over. Zigzag and Ainsley were the first to serve themselves, with Amadeus and Leo trailing them. Winston oversaw the affair from the doorway but appeared to be absorbed with checking his watch. He finally followed me in the line for food.

The pasta and soup looked good. I skipped the fish. The lodge had somehow managed to acquire green vegetables and fruit despite their distance from civilization and it made me wonder just how much time travel was involved in the food prep. The wine on the table was pricey too. No expense spared.

I'd helped myself to the bread basket and had already begun on the salad before having to engage in conversation. Roman Amadeus seemed intent on charming the lovely Ainsley, but he left enough space in the conversation that she soon turned toward me.

"I hear you've made a real name for yourself as a detective. You solve any cases I might have heard of?"

"Doubtful," I said. "It's mostly work for linears. Quick jump back in time can solve most problems. Easy money."

"And that's your chronometer?" She gestured to the watch-like device on my wrist. "I've never seen one before."

"They're usually reserved for friends of the inventor," I said. "Though Roman seems to have acquired one."

Roman gave a grin. "Not much that can't be had for the right price." He pushed up the edge of his suit jacket and displayed the concentric rings that selected the various time destinations. "And I find it an elegant solution to getting around off-Grid."

"I got to use a Temprovibe Two once," Ainsley said. "But they've gotten so expensive. I have to travel with someone else who has one now."

"What about you, Zigzag?" Roman inquired. "What are you wearing tonight?"

"Came by the gate. Didn't think I'd need alternate options."

"Indeed," Roman replied. "Leo felt the same." He turned toward me. "It seems only you and I are temporally untethered."

27

"Have somewhere else to be?" I asked. "Don't let us keep you."

But before Roman could answer, the door to the dining room opened and Mary Hurst entered, her shoulders damp from mist. Her boots were caked with mud and she wore a pained expression on her face.

Winston Carlisle immediately rose to greet her. But when he noticed the state she was in, he rushed over. They spoke in hushed tones and the more Hurst said, the less Carlisle seemed to like the news.

I'd finished my meal by the time Carlisle addressed the group.

"My apologies. There has been an unexpected delay. As you know, we are anticipating the arrival of our courier, Logan Tyler. But it seems the time gate has been moved."

"What for?" Leo asked.

Carlisle threw up his hands. "It wasn't part of the plans. And with the courier due to arrive shortly, it's imperative that we locate the gate and ensure it is in a safe location for their arrival."

"I was told there was no one else on the island," Roman said.

"There isn't," Carlisle replied.

"Are you suggesting it got up and moved on its own?" Roman's tone had lost some of its charm.

"Ms. Hurst returned to the gate shortly after the arrival of Mr. Travers, but she found the truck and gate were gone."

"Gone?" Ainsley asked.

It was a strange claim to make if we were really alone.

I stood. "Ms. Hurst, did you notice tracks from the truck being moved?"

"I'm fine being called Mary," she said. "And yes. I followed the tracks for a while but they were twisted. Like someone was either lost or deliberately confused them. I couldn't make any sense of it."

"Are we stuck here?" Ainsley asked. "How are we supposed to get home?"

"I'm just as concerned as you are," Winston replied. "But there is no one else on this island and what Ms. Hurst is describing sounds absolutely impossible. Perhaps she was in error as to the location. The evening fog can be disorienting."

Mary Hurst raised an eyebrow. She didn't seem like the disoriented type, but it had to be looked into.

"I'll check it out," I said. "My AI was running a location app when I arrived. I should be able to retrace my steps to the gate site easily enough. What time is the courier due to arrive?"

Winston checked his watch. "Only twenty minutes from now."

"We should all search," Roman interjected. He rose from his chair. "Leo and I will help comb the area."

I surveyed him skeptically, but in this situation we needed all the help we could get. If the courier arrived and the gate wasn't set up in a safe location, they could easily be injured or worse.

"I'll get changed," Ainsley said and disappeared through the hallway door.

"Yes. We'll all look," Carlisle confirmed.

Only Zigzag had remained seated. She hadn't finished her meal and she seemed to be regretting that fact. But as the rest of us made our way to the door, she rose to follow. I noticed she still didn't meet my eye.

"Mary, I'd like you to come with me and describe what you saw," I said.

She scratched her neck. "Can't one of you people just bounce back in time to see what happened?" she asked.

"Possibly. But we need to know more about what we're looking for. If we chose the wrong moment to go back to we could hurt the timeline or wind up riding an ontological paradox to the afterlife. It's a little more complicated than it seems. Let's start by trying to find it the old fashioned way."

She sized me up. "Temperature is dropping. You'll need a coat." She moved to the hall closet and reached inside.

When she returned she was carrying a flashlight and a knee-length, gray, wool coat with a navy quilted liner. "A previous guest left this."

I recognized it immediately as the coat I'd been wearing in the photo from Rosen. My stomach gave a twinge. Felt like I was aboard a train with no brakes.

But it was good to know I was one step closer to whatever future I was careening toward. I shrugged into the coat, accepted the flashlight from Mary, and made for the door.

CHAPTER 7

Fog had settled heavily on the island.

I descended the steps from the wide wooden porch and stared into the night. My flashlight hindered as much as it helped. The fog refracted the light back at me and all I could make out was wet grass that stretched a half dozen yards before it vanished in the gray.

Chatter from behind me announced the others. Winston Carlisle had a rain slicker on and carried a lantern as he clomped down the steps. Mary Hurst preceded him, her expression unreadable.

Roman Amadeus struck a gallant figure in an expensive black dress coat better suited for a visit to the orchestra than the outdoors. But I supposed style had no borders. His thug bodyguard, Leo, was on the opposite end of the fashion spectrum, garbed in a washed-out New York Yankees hoodie complete with ketchup and mustard stains. His gun made an obvious bulge in his waistband.

Ainsley Parker was the last to join the sortie. She'd changed into a running top and leggings that managed to leave as little to the imagination as the cocktail dress had. But she at least had a puffy pink coat to cover up with. Her sneakers had glow-in-the-dark laces.

"You have a plan for this search?" Amadeus asked. Everyone was looking at me.

I turned to Mary Hurst. "You know this island best. Where is there to go from here in a truck besides the lodge?"

"The old Coast Guard Station near the airfield, but that's a fair piece of driving and you'd have to come back past the lodge to get that way. We'd have heard it." Hurst pulled a paper map from her jacket and unfolded it. She jabbed a finger at a spot in the northeast corner of the island. "We're near Addison Creek now. Scout Canyon. That's Holtz Bay. Everything you might call developed is southeast toward Massacre Bay. Just the one road to get there. But the road is that way and the truck tracks I saw go that way." She pointed west.

"What's in that direction?" I asked.

"Whole lot of fuck all."

At least she didn't mince words.

"All right. Let's follow the tracks. We'll have to move fast. We have any other vehicles handy?"

"Four-wheeler at the utility shed and a Suburban here at the lodge. But the Suburban's no good for off-road on this terrain. We'd roll it."

"How far is the utility shed?"

"Eighth of a mile the other way."

"Better get the four-wheeler. Meet us down at the gate site. Seems like that old truck with a heavy load like a time gate couldn't have gotten far in these hills."

"Not in this weather either," she said.

I nodded. "We'll head to the site of the gate on foot and check the scene. Meet us with the four-wheeler. We can fan out from there and search." Mary turned on her heel and walked into the fog in the direction of the utility shed. I reached into my pocket and pulled out my sunglasses. Slipping them on, I tapped the power button. "Waldo, activate low-light and Breadcrumbs."

The lenses of my glasses illuminated a path ahead of me showing the trail I'd taken from the gate on my arrival.

The others were still waiting for a cue. "Stick close," I said and led the way.

In a matter of moments, the lodge was swallowed up by fog, and after a hundred yards even its lights were indiscernible.

I kept a steady pace, quick, but careful of my footwork. Turning an ankle would be easy on the uneven ground. I paused briefly around midway to the gate and checked behind me. "Everyone still with us?"

I could only see Carlisle. He looked behind him. Another light bobbed through the fog and Ainsley appeared, followed closely by Amadeus.

"Where's your buddy?" I asked.

"Needed to water the grass. He's a big boy. He'll catch up."

We pressed on.

It was another five minutes of brisk walking till we reached the end of the trail.

If it hadn't been for the tire tracks and the proximity of the ocean noise, we could have been ten yards from the lodge again. Everything was fog. But I trusted Waldo more than my senses.

"You're sure this is the place?" Winston asked. He peered past me to the south. "Feels like we haven't gone far enough."

"This is it," I said. "Truck was parked right there."

The grass was mashed down from the tires and there was a broad swath where the time gate doorway had rested.

"Keys were kept in the truck?" I asked.

Carlisle nodded. Made sense. Mary knew everyone on the island and had no reason to suspect theft. Not like there was anywhere to sell a stolen vehicle.

Ainsley appeared at my elbow, breathing heavily. I caught a whiff of cherry lip gloss. "What now?"

Amadeus checked his watch. "Our courier is supposed to arrive any minute."

There was no sign of Mary and the four-wheeler.

"I'll check toward the water," Winston said. "There's level ground down there where someone could set up the gate." He was breathing hard but he looked determined.

"Tracks go this way," I contended, pointing west.

"Yet they could circle back in any direction," he said. "In this fog, how can you tell?"

He wasn't wrong.

"Let's fan out. Move as quick as you can but stay in earshot. You don't see anything within a hundred yards, circle back to me. I'll be following the tracks directly."

The others pointed their flashlights into the fog in other directions. "Let's not waste time," Amadeus said, and marched into the fog.

Ainsley gave me one more glance, then forged into the grass to my right. I shone my flashlight along the path of crushed grass and broke into a jog.

I'd only made it about seventy five yards when I heard a familiar buzz. Uphill there was a change to the color of the fog. It brightened as if backlit. A brilliant flash permeated the mist and made it glow bluish purple. The time gate was on.

I cut through the grass and ran hard uphill. It was tough going. I hit an incline that pitched sharply upward and I lost sight of the glow entirely as I struggled up it. When I gained the top of the hill the fog had lost its brilliance. Whoever had come through the gate was here. But I had no idea where.

"Waldo. Can you orient me to where that flash was?"

My sunglasses display illuminated the place the flash had come from. I broke into a jog again.

"The refracted light from the gate event left a twenty percent margin of error in my estimated course," Waldo said.

"Noted," I panted.

It was another ninety seconds and a hundred yards till I found the time gate. The old truck was there, parked on a level patch of ground at the base of another hill. Abandoned. Someone had activated the hoist and set the gate on the ground for use but there was no one in sight. I spun in place, peering in every direction.

"You see anybody?"

"There appears to be no one near the vehicle," Waldo replied.

Then came the gunshot. I ducked instinctively, dropping my flashlight and going for my gun.

A second gunshot echoed through the night.

The sound was muffled, somewhere to my right. Nothing impacted near me. I had my Stinger 1911 out of its holster and unlocked. I aimed it into the fog and moved a few steps away from where my flashlight lay on the ground, just in case someone was aiming for it.

"Give me something, Waldo," I hissed.

"The shots came from the northeast. Perhaps two hundred yards."

I moved that way with slow, deliberate steps. I listened hard.

Then came the screams. Ainsley.

I ran.

CHAPTER 8

I nearly collided with Ainsley in the fog.

She shrieked again when she saw me, then gasped. She was standing alone, the glow of her flashlight a tiny bubble of light in the mist.

"Greyson. Thank God."

She rushed for me, panting hard. It looked like she might hug me, but she sprang back when she realized I was holding a gun.

"It's okay," I said. I pulled my sunglasses from my face and tucked them away. "What did you see?"

She shivered involuntarily, her big eyes watering. "I saw someone. In the fog." She shone her light northward. "Someone got shot. That way."

I looked the way she was pointing but saw nothing. Just more high grass. More fog. There was a trail through the grass from the south where Ainsley had found her way here, and another where I'd cut across to find her. We made a new path now as I walked the way she'd indicated. Ainsley reached out and grasped my arm, clinging to me. I paused and took her right hand with my left, keeping my gun aimed into the fog with my right.

"It's all right. Stick close."

We walked. Ainsley holding the light. Me with the gun.

Rushing footsteps sounded ahead. Someone moving toward us. Closing fast.

"Hey!" I shouted. "Hold it right there!" I let go of Ainsley and took a two-handed grip on my Stinger.

The footsteps stopped. As we edged forward, Ainsley's flashlight illuminated the figure in the mist. She stood like a statue with her hands up. "Don't shoot."

"Zigzag?"

She was dressed in a black rain slicker and knee-high boots. Where the hell had she come from?

She moved a hand across her face, shielding her eyes from the light and blinking.

"I saw someone get shot," Ainsley said. "Did you see it too?"

Zigzag was staring at me, her eyes on my gun. I realized I was still aiming it at her and lowered it. She appeared to be unarmed. "What happened?" I asked.

But she only stared. Might have been shock. She held a flashlight but it was off. I moved past Zigzag, following the path she'd come by and scanning for more threats. Ainsley hurried to catch up, casting a nervous glance back toward Zigzag.

Ahead there was a patch of grass that had been matted down in a swath. It appeared as though something had been dragged through it. The grass was slick with blood.

Twenty yards farther on, the trail ended at a level patch of rock and gravel. It was like whoever had been walking here just vanished. Or they doubled back.

I kept an eye out for any sign of the shooter, but saw no one.

Retracing my steps, I found Ainsley staring at the slick grass. "That's a lot of blood. You think they're dead?"

"Hard to say."

Zigzag was still with us, albeit at a distance. She didn't seem inclined to get any closer. Probably best. If this was indeed a crime scene, we might already be disturbing clues as to the nature of the shooting.

But if someone was shot, where were they?

Engine noise permeated the fog. The four-wheeler. South of us.

"Over here!" Ainsley shouted. She waved her light.

The vehicle idled briefly, then grew louder as it turned our way. Finally the light made an appearance as more than just a dull glow. The twin beams cut a path ahead of the vehicle and blinded us all till Mary turned at an angle. She cut the engine. Leo was on the back of the four-wheeler, looking not the least bit happy about it.

"Found this one wandering around by his lonesome," Mary said. "Where are the others?"

"Coming!" Winston shouted from down the hill. Presently he appeared out of the fog, winded but otherwise intact. He stopped when he saw the bloody grass. "Good God. Who is hurt?"

"I saw someone get shot," Ainsley said. "Right here."

"Who?" Mary asked.

"I don't know. I just saw two people in the fog, and one of them shot the other one."

Winston looked appalled. "Did you see a face?"

Ainsley shook her head. "They were too far away."

I looked down the hill toward where I'd found Ainsley, but I couldn't make it out from here. "Did they have lights when you saw them?"

Ainsley furrowed her brow. "Lights?"

"For you to see that far."

"Oh," she replied. "I guess they must have."

"Anyone see Amadeus?" I looked around for the mobster. He was the only one of us still unaccounted for.

"Last I saw he was with you," Winston replied.

I frowned. "What time is it?"

Winston took a pocket watch from his vest. "Eight-forty. Our courier should have been here by now."

"Could be hurt," Mary said. "Hurt bad, judging from that blood. Doubt they got far. We ought to look."

"But there is someone shooting," Ainsley said, drawing closer to me again. "What if they want to shoot more of us?"

"We're sitting ducks as it is now," I said. "The poor visibility might be a hindrance, but only if they're keeping their distance."

Something moved behind me and I spun, leveling my gun at the figure approaching through the grass.

"It's me, Greyson." Roman Amadeus emerged from the fog with a flashlight in one hand and a pistol in the other. I kept mine aimed at him. He stopped.

"Surely you don't think I was the one shooting," he said. "I was the farthest from the action."

"With a gun," I said.

"Shall I be the one to state the obvious?" he said and flicked his flashlight beam till it illuminated me. My Stinger in particular. "And we're not the only ones."

Ainsley gasped.

I turned to see what she was looking at and found Leo pointing his cannon of a pistol at me. Looked like a 50 Caliber Desert Eagle from where I was standing, but mine wasn't the preferred angle to be studying it from.

I still didn't take my gun sights off Amadeus.

"We should calm ourselves," Winston pleaded. "We're all friends here."

"Mary, will you do me a favor?" I asked.

Mary Hurst took a cautious step closer.

"I'd like you to walk over to Mr. Amadeus's weapon and smell it for us. If it's been fired in the last few minutes you should be able to tell."

"What about him?" she asked, indicating Leo.

"We'll check him last. The gun we heard in the fog wasn't loud enough to be his, but we'll do our due diligence."

When Mary Hurst approached Amadeus, he acquiesced to her inspecting his gun. I suspected he played along largely because Leo still had me covered.

Mary Hurst took his pistol and sniffed it. She shook her head. "Doesn't smell like gun smoke."

"Your turn," Roman said and collected his weapon from Mary. He didn't bother to raise it. He merely held it loosely in one hand.

Mary crossed to me and I tipped my pistol forward. She inclined her head over the hammer and took a whiff. She looked at Amadeus and shook her head. I lowered my gun to thigh level.

The others watched in curiosity as Mary made her way to Leo, but I knew what she'd find. He hadn't fired that cannon. They'd have heard it halfway to the mainland. But he seemed the most reluctant to stand down.

"Leo," Amadeus commanded.

Leo finally lowered the gun and allowed Mary to examine it. She turned toward me and shook her head.

Winston sighed. "So we've cleared that up. It wasn't one of us."

"We've only resolved it wasn't one of these three guns. And only for the moment," I said.

Winston screwed up his brow. "You think there are more weapons on the island?"

"I think this is the most dangerous group of people you've ever hosted at your lodge, Winston. And even if no one here has shot someone yet, it doesn't prove they won't. We've got lots of time."

CHAPTER 9

A fire roared in the stone hearth of the drawing room. We'd gathered there after our excursion in the fog.

Winston Carlisle was attempting to wear a hole through the rug with his pacing. He occasionally threw worried glances toward the windows.

The rest of us were mostly stationary, and keeping wary distances from one another.

"I just don't know what's happening," Winston moaned. "All the planning. All the secrecy. No one knew the gate schedule except Mary and me. Nobody." If he had more hair I suspect he might try pulling it out. Fortunately his mostly bald head left little in danger.

I'd mixed myself another old fashioned but was taking my time drinking it. Amadeus had likewise poured himself a cocktail, and despite our previous standoff, seemed generally nonplussed about the situation.

We'd loaded up the time gate and returned it with the truck to the lodge. The truck was now parked downstairs. I could see a corner of it from my seat at the bar.

Zigzag sat on a chaise lounge with a tablet in her lap and was analyzing the data she'd downloaded from the time gate's control unit.

"There was more than one jump since Greyson arrived," she said at last. "At least one at seven forty-five, and another at eight-thirty."

"What do you mean by 'at least one?'" I asked. "You aren't sure?"

"Frequencies are a bit scrambled. Might be nothing. But that happens sometimes if two departure destinations and arrival times are really similar. It's hard to tell the jumps apart. Might be only one there. I don't know. The one at eight-thirty was easy to decipher because it clearly came from a departure point in the past."

"That would be our courier," Winston said. "Logan Tyler. The time concurs with their scheduled arrival time."

Zigzag shrugged. "Could be. I'm just telling you what you asked to know."

"Yes. Thank you." Winston wrung his hands some more. "And now we have no courier. Should we be out there searching again?"

Leo DeRossi was picking at his nails with a pocket knife. He didn't seem to be paying attention to the conversation. Ainsley had taken up residence in one corner of the sofa, and it was in danger of swallowing her if she pressed herself any farther into the cushions. "I'm not going back out there," she said. "Didn't you hear her? Someone showed up unannounced and could still be out there right now waiting for us. The smart move is to stay here, right?"

I studied the group. Seven of us, and one courier missing in the fog. Plus one visitor who jumped in from the future. I had too many questions to make sense of it yet.

"I think it's time I had the whole story on this project," I said. "I wasn't expecting a party when I got here. Rosen gave the impression this rendezvous would be low key. Who lied to her?"

"The number of members involved in the operation was always to be kept private," Winston said. "At the request of Mr. Weintraub. No one misled Rosen."

"Where is this Weintraub?" I asked. "If it's his deal, why isn't he here?"

"Something I'd like to know as well," Amadeus said. "Considering he's used a great deal of my resources."

Winston Carlisle looked uncomfortable. "I received a message from Mr. Weintraub that he was unavoidably detained. He did not give a reason. But I assured him we would be more than capable of handling the reception of the artifact."

Something didn't add up. If Weintraub was a time traveler, "last-minute" plan changes shouldn't have been a deterrent.

I focused my attention on Winston. "Remind me of your involvement, again?"

He looked offended. "I'm the historian. You think a recovery agent would have had any chance of locating the Warsaw Pendulum without my research?"

I sipped my drink, then slid off my stool. "You're the acquisition research. Rosen was the bankroll." I turned toward Amadeus. "Fashion consultant?"

"I provided the time gates for the job," he said dryly. "An expensive contribution, I might add."

I nodded. "One gate here and at least one in the past. Something portable no doubt. But you'd need someone to program your gates for you." I looked to Zigzag. "Someone smart enough to get around any sticky permitting problems. Maybe someone who owes you." Zigzag narrowed her eyes but didn't contradict me. I finally landed on Ainsley. She met my gaze.

"I'm just the actuary," she said.

"You mentioned risk assessment."

She nodded. "I make sure it's a good investment before the club gets involved. A wealthy client like Rosen might seem like an easy person to say yes to, but someone still has to check."

"Because wealthy clients like Rosen also have teams of litigious lawyers ready to eat you alive?"

"You get it," Ainsley said. "Maybe you should join my team."

"So the ACC coordinates recovery projects for its wealthy members. Do actuaries always tag along for the recovery phase?"

"Mr. Carlisle thought it would be educational."

I looked at Winston. He put his palms up. "And it should have been. We should all be drinking wine and examining a priceless historical artifact at the moment."

I set my drink down and crossed my arms. "Okay. We have a team invested in this acquisition. But the big payday doesn't happen till the courier shows up with the pendulum. Who benefits if it never shows up?"

"The Nazis?" Leo offered. He had finally tuned into the conversation. For what it was worth.

"Let's try someone more recent," I said.

Amadeus flicked idly at a bit of old candle wax on the mantle. "Anyone in this group has a motive for theft, if that's what you're getting at. The pendulum unlocks the arrival location of the accumulated Warsaw treasure."

I frowned. "Musty records. Old family candlesticks. I get the sentimental value to a family like Rosen's, who lost relatives in the Holocaust, but what value is that to us?"

"If that's all it contains, then you must be right," Amadeus replied. But he didn't sound convincing. It was obvious he knew something I didn't about this treasure and he wasn't trying hard to conceal it. I didn't particularly like that. Or him.

"Has everyone forgotten our bigger problem?" Ainsley said. "Someone just got shot. We should be getting the hell out of here." She pushed herself off the couch. "I'm getting my stuff. Which one of you is going to set up the time gate?"

"You're not leaving."

We all turned to look at Zigzag.

Ainsley bristled. "You're going to try to stop me?"

Zigzag didn't blink. "No one can leave. The gate is locked. We're stuck here. Better get used to it."

CHAPTER 10

"You've got to be shitting me," Ainsley said. Her cheeks were red with fury.

If Zigzag was moved by her outburst, she didn't show it.

"The time gate has been locked since the beginning. No departures. Only arrivals, for twenty-four hours. That's how Weintraub wanted it set up. It's a safety precaution to prevent someone from stealing the pendulum."

"Safety precaution?" Ainsley fumed. "How is it safe to trap us here with a killer?"

"It's actually standard protocol," Winston acknowledged. "It's why we selected the lodge. A remote place. Keeps everyone honest. It was meant to avoid the occurrence we now find ourselves in."

"So a thief, if there is one, would have had to use other means to get off the island," I said.

"Good luck with that," Mary Hurst said. She had taken a seat at the sideboard and was cracking walnuts with a silver nutcracker. "Boat won't be back for a week."

"No planes. No boats. Now no time gate," I said. "A handy little thief trap. But someone could still get off the island with a chronometer."

All the eyes in the room turned to Roman Amadeus.

He blinked slowly. Then looked at me with half-lidded eyes. "There is one on your wrist as well, Greyson."

I glanced down at my chronometer. I ignored his implication. "But you'd still need an anchor. Something not from here to give you a place to jump to." It was a limitation to the way we traveled that couldn't be ignored. Jumping through time only gets you so far, if what you really need is a way to jump through space. Anchor-based time travel meant you needed to be in contact with something not traveling through time while you jumped in order to stay affixed to the planet.

"You are welcome to search my belongings," Amadeus replied. "You will find no pendulums."

"Could have jumped out already. Dropped the pendulum, and come back."

"Hi Pot, my name is Kettle."

He had a point. It was only our word against the other's that neither of us had jumped away with the pendulum and come back. But I knew for a fact I hadn't.

"Max range on my chronometer is about ten years," I said. "I jumped in from farther than that with the gate. And I don't have any non-local anchors to get me out."

Amadeus shrugged. "You'll find I'm in the same circumstance."

"One of you could jump forward in time to when the gate is unlocked," Leo offered. "Right?"

"You could jump us forward now!" Ainsley said. "Get us out of here."

Amadeus crossed his arms. "And leave without the job done? Somehow I don't think Greyson will do that."

I thought about the photo in my pocket. The photo that hadn't been taken yet. If I left now it would create a paradox.

Possibly alter the timeline. That wasn't an option for me. Amadeus seemed to know it.

But Leo's comment highlighted another particularly thorny problem. Amadeus wouldn't have needed a time gate to jump back and kill the courier either. He could have used his chronometer. But if he did, it meant I was no closer to knowing who had made the jump with the gate.

"Seems to me any one of you could have done it," Mary Hurst said. "What's to keep someone from waiting till tomorrow when this gate unlocks, jumping back then and doing the shooting?"

No one had an answer for her. It was a valid question.

"Looks like we find ourselves in a standoff again," Amadeus said. "If the only people who know about the job are here, then it stands to reason one of us is the pendulum thief. I, for one, don't intend to leave until we recover it."

No one said anything for a long time. Finally Ainsley broke the silence. "So no one is getting me out of here?"

Amadeus and I were busy glaring at each other.

"Then I'm calling the cops," Ainsley said. "Someone has to do something."

That jarred me from my stare down with Roman. She had a point.

"Zigzag, you said the gate was locked for departures. What about arrivals?"

Zigzag looked to Ainsley and back to me. "Yeah. Someone else could come in if we got them the gate coordinates."

I turned to Winston. "This place have a tachyon pulse transmitter we can use to get a message out?"

He nodded. "It's upstairs. I can set it up in the hall."

"Grab it," I said.

Winston hurried out.

"Who exactly do you intend to call?" Amadeus asked.

"I have a detective friend at Time Crimes," I said. "She'd be an obvious choice."

"A little too obvious perhaps?" he asked. "Is this the same friend who was staking out my club in a surveillance van the night we first met?"

I frowned.

"Did you think I wasn't aware of the activities of the Temporal Crimes Investigation Division in New York, Greyson? Pardon me if I don't rush to call a woman actively trying to imprison me."

"If you have nothing to hide, what does it matter?" I asked.

"So you wouldn't mind if we call a different agent. How about, what's his name . . . Agent Baker? I hear he knows you too."

Amadeus had done his research. I had to give him that. Agent Baker hated my guts and he obviously knew it.

The idea of Baker getting a chance to make me a suspect in a murder investigation made my skin twitch.

"Fine. Someone neutral then. There are plenty of other Time Crimes agents."

There had to be a few who didn't hate me yet.

"I'll call," Ainsley said. "I'm not going to just sit here and listen to you two argue about it." She moved toward the hall. Winston came lumbering down the stairs with the transmitter in his arms. It took some set up, but after a few minutes he had the thing plugged in and operable. Ainsley punched in the coordinates of the presiding Time Crimes office and the tachyon pulse transmitter clicked to life. She cradled the handset with both hands as she waited.

I finished my drink while it connected. Someone picked up.

"Yes. I need to report a shooting."

The conversation took less than five minutes. Midway

through she consulted with Zigzag to get the coordinates for our time gate.

When she finally set the handset down, she turned to address us. "They're sending two agents to get statements. They want to arrive later tonight."

"Did they give you the agent's names?" Amadeus asked.

"Yes. They said their names are Fallgrave and Osborne."

I raised my eyebrows. "Constantine Fallgrave?"

"I guess so," she said. "Is that important?"

"No. I just thought he'd retired. He's one of the best detectives in the business. He literally wrote the book on temporal investigation."

"So you shouldn't have any complaints about his methods," Amadeus said.

My shoulders relaxed. "No. Fallgrave is good. He'll get it sorted."

The sense of relief was palpable in the room. A solution. I didn't mind that it wasn't going to come from me. Someone else could resolve this mess. All I had to do was wait till they showed up.

"I'd like to suggest something," Winston said, "if it is agreeable to you gentlemen." He still looked pensive. "It's just the issue of those . . . chronometers." He glanced furtively between Amadeus and I. "You can understand why they make the rest of us uncomfortable in this situation."

"What are you suggesting?" I asked.

"Guarding them. For safekeeping. Just till this investigation can resolve itself."

Amadeus frowned. "Why should we trust *you* with them?"

"You won't have to," Winston said, his hands waving off the concern. "We have a safe on premises. Time locked. We can secure them till tomorrow and even I wouldn't be able to get to them. No one would."

Amadeus and I exchanged glances.

I didn't like the idea of being stuck in linear time if something went south, but the fact that Time Crimes was on the way gave me some assurance. Amadeus with a chronometer on his wrist presented too many variables. He didn't seem to like the idea too much either. Another plus.

If this compromise meant taking Roman off the board, it seemed a worthwhile sacrifice.

Winston waited expectantly.

"Okay," I said. "But I'm keeping my gun."

CHAPTER 11

Three people watched me deposit my chronometer in the wall safe in the library. Winston and Amadeus were necessary to the operation. I wasn't sure why Mary Hurst had come along but she followed the process with a keen eye. Maybe Winston had wanted a witness. The time gate was due to unlock at 8pm the following night. He set the time lock on the safe for 7:55pm.

When both mine and Roman's chronometers were safely inside and locked, Winston sighed. "There. And we can all have peace of mind." He looked visibly relieved. "We'll leave it to the authorities."

Roman had assumed a stone-faced expression. Whatever he was thinking, it was locked away in its own vault. I had concerns of my own, but the weight of the gun at my waist made me feel a little better about them.

We returned to the drawing room overlooking the hillside and found it vacant with the exception of Leo.

"Where have the young ladies gone?" Winston asked.

Leo shrugged.

A wonder his conversation skills hadn't kept the women's interest.

"Someone will need to set up the time gate for the agents' arrival," I said.

"I can manage that," Winston replied. "With a bit of help from Miss Zhang, once I find her."

"I've got food to prep for the morning," Mary Hurst interjected. "Especially now that we'll have more guests. I'd best get on that."

The conversation had a forced tone. We were making an effort to ignore the fact that someone had recently been shot. None of us were especially convincing. Winston and Mary departed.

Roman Amadeus and his goon weren't my idea of good company, so I left the sitting room as well, making my way back to the library. According to Ainsley, we had some time till the agents would arrive. I couldn't have said why they wanted the delay but they were calling the shots now. Not my problem.

I contemplated the spines of the books in the library. But after a few moments I realized I wasn't even reading them. My brain was too full. Too many questions.

"You seem restless," Waldo said in my ear.

"This night has been a puzzle. Has me curious."

"One of your dominant character traits."

"Let's do some process of elimination. You game?"

I fished in my pockets and came up with a small notepad and pen. Getting the thoughts out of my head sometimes helped.

"You think the shooter is in this lodge," Waldo said.

"Don't you?"

"Insufficient data."

"I'm going to make wild assumptions then."

The armchairs in the library were cushy. Deep and tall. I chose one that faced the door and was a reasonable distance from the windows. I set my Stinger 1911 on the table next to me. Didn't hurt to have it handy.

I settled into the chair, then took a long breath and stared at a blank page of my notepad.

"Seven people." I listed each of the other guests' names in black ink.

Simply staring at the name Roman Amadeus made me want to pin him as the shooter. So I would.

"Roman did it."

"That was fast," Waldo said. "Case closed?"

But I had to admit it didn't make sense yet. Roman didn't need to get his hands dirty. He had a thug who did dirty work for him. We'd all been in the fog.

"Who could have physically reached the location of the shooting from the time we last laid eyes on them?" I asked.

"Based on the average physical condition of the persons in question and the terrain limitations, it would be possible for any of your suspects to reach the site with varying degrees of ease."

Balls. I'd need some tougher criteria.

"Who had the longest and shortest windows of opportunity?"

"Miss Parker had the shortest window and Miss Zhang had the longest."

"Huh."

Ainsley seemed easy to rule out. She'd been with me most of the time. But I came upon her after the shooting. She could have thrown away a gun, though her outfit had left few places to hide one when she left the lodge. Yoga pants don't support holsters well, and that puffy jacket looked like it was made of cotton candy.

Zigzag was closer to the site of the shooting, and I'd never even seen her leave the lodge. She knew how to handle a gun. I'd known her for years but trusted her about as far as I could throw her. I put a line under her name.

"What about Leo?"

"Mr. DeRossi had the third longest window of opportunity after Miss Zhang and Ms. Mary Hurst."

Roman had said Leo was taking a leak, but that could have been covering for him while he diverted to the new site of the gate. He hadn't fired that Desert Eagle, but who's to say he didn't have a second gun he threw away?

"I need a drink."

I picked my gun back up.

Walking back into the drawing room, I found it empty. Luckily the bourbon bottle was still mostly full. I made a drink and took it for a walk.

The lodge was bigger than it looked. The drawing room was the largest feature facing the coastline, but there were plenty of other spaces. The dining room adjoined an expansive kitchen. I could hear Mary Hurst rattling around in there prepping meals for the next day.

A linear like Hurst had to be the lowest on my list of suspects for the shooting. Someone had come through that time gate ahead of Logan Tyler. If Tyler was dead, it means someone moved a body too. Mary Hurst was tough. I had no doubt she could manage the terrain and use a gun. Any woman who made a trek to this remote island on her own was made of grit and nails. But a killer? I had a hard time seeing her motive. She also lacked an escape route. Who murders someone knowing it will take a week for a boat to come for a getaway?

There were several bedrooms along the wing of the lodge I was entering. I paused near one and heard a cough that sounded like Winston. The old man wasn't high on my list either. But he was sturdy. He could physically manage hauling a body. He seemed too bookish to be spending many days at the shooting range, but people can surprise you. Of all the guests, he seemed the most distraught about the way events were unfolding. It's possible it was all an act, but my gut said no. I knew a lot of liars.

If Winston was hiding a murderous streak, he was a better actor than any criminal I'd met.

I'd met a lot of criminals.

The corridor ended with a door to a sort of atrium. The door was unlocked but I couldn't locate a light switch. Looks like it might have once housed birds, but if there were any in here now, they were asleep or dead.

I sipped my drink and turned around. There was a door here that led outside, so I made my way back to the library by way of the wrap-around wooden porch. The wind had picked up off the water. I caught the briefest glimpse of the stars before the next wave of clouds obscured it. The wind made me shiver. I found the outside doors to the library unlocked and remedied the situation by getting back inside. I flipped the lock shut.

I looked out over the gray, fog-covered landscape and nearly spit my drink out when I saw a light blink somewhere in the distance. I opened the door again and stepped back onto the porch. But by the time I reached the railing, the light was gone. Staring into the darkness did no good. The fog was shifting in the wind, but after a solid minute of watching, the light failed to reappear.

I noted the time. Just past ten.

Maybe I'd imagined it.

The night air sent a chill down my spine. I retreated indoors again and relocked the door. I made my way to my bedroom and was surprised to find it locked as well. I double-checked the knob but it definitely wasn't moving.

I stared at the door jamb and listened.

What the hell.

Fortunately I had a tool for this occasion. I slipped a hand into my blazer jacket pocket and extracted the room key I'd been given. I inserted the key slowly, eased the door knob unlatched, then drew my gun before pushing the door open slowly with one finger of my drink hand. The lights were on in the room but no one was in evidence. That is, until I made my way around the corner of the bed and looked into the bathroom. The reflection in the mirror shrieked and spun around, revealing that her bathrobe had been covering panties and nothing else. Ainsley Parker clutched at the edges of her robe and pulled them across her bare breasts. "Don't you knock?"

Good gracious.

My evening had just gotten a lot more interesting.

CHAPTER 12

I put my gun away.

"What are you doing in my room, Ainsley?"

The young woman's hair was still soaking wet, so I knew part of the answer.

"I thought you'd be back sooner. I got tired of waiting so I decided to jump in the shower." After securing her robe, She pulled another towel off the rack and began dabbing at her hair.

"No shower in your room?"

She gave me an exasperated eye-roll. "There is a killer on this island. If they are trying to get me, my room will be the first place they'll look."

I could admit that my shower would not have been high on my list of places to expect to find her.

I shrugged out of my blazer and hung it in the closet. Then I leaned against the bureau as Ainsley began brushing out her long auburn hair.

"Why my room?" I said.

"You're a cop. You have a gun. No one is going to mess with you. So I decided your room was the safest place on the island right now."

"I'm a private cop."

"Potato, potato. I don't care." She continued brushing.

"It's potato, po-tah-to."

"What?"

"The saying. You pronounce the second one differently."

She wrinkled her nose. "Who the hell says po-tah-to?"

I shrugged.

"That's stupid." She waved the hairbrush. "I'm trying to say they're the same. Potato, potato. You're a cop."

I sighed. "You know what, your way actually makes sense."

She perched a hand on her hip. "I know how this looks. And it's not that I like being the vulnerable female, you know?"

"I didn't call you vulnerable."

"But I am, right? I can't help it. If I'm in a situation at work or just out and about, I can hold my own just fine. It's not my fault that I'm at a disadvantage when it comes to fighting off killers on islands. You're the biggest and strongest and you have a gun and you have all the advantages I don't. It's practical to stick with you."

"I get it."

"And I know that women are supposed to not need men to fight their battles for them anymore or whatever, but in this *situation*, that's bullshit. I can't argue gender equality with a psycho. It's not like they are going to suddenly not murder me just because I brought up the inequality of the circumstances. And I get that I let myself in uninvited and it looks bad or whatever, but if it's either that or getting murdered, I choose this."

"Ainsley, would you like to stay in my room for a while to avoid being murdered?"

She took her hand off her hip. "Yes. Thank you. That would be nice." She went back into the bathroom.

The bedroom door was still hanging open so I walked over

and closed it, then twisted the lock. Ainsley didn't seem like she was planning to depart anytime soon.

Either the drinks had caught up to me or this conversation had. I felt tired. I kicked off my boots and sprawled on the king bed. Ainsley walked out of the bathroom again, still brushing her hair, and eyed me. "You really think someone died out there tonight?" The tie of her robe had loosened from all her vigorous brushing and the increasingly generous view was distracting, but I tried to focus on her question.

"Someone got hurt pretty badly at minimum. It was a lot of blood."

She screwed up her face in disgust. "I can't think about it. I just want to get out of here." She marched back into the bathroom and fussed with her hair some more. When she came back out she was wearing a T-shirt but was still in her panties. She had also obviously forgone a bra. I couldn't say the outfit change was any less distracting. But if she was in any way conscious of what it was doing to my concentration, she didn't let on.

She pulled back the bed covers on the opposite side of the bed and slipped under them. "I'm going to stay here until the other cops show up. If I fall asleep, don't leave without waking me up, okay?"

"Make yourself at home, I guess." I adjusted a pillow behind my head and pulled the gun out from under my waist. I set the holster and weapon on my nightstand. When I laid back again, I found Ainsley watching me. It seemed like she'd gotten closer.

"You have a girlfriend?" Her voice had softened. Calmer now.

"No." An image of Heavens popped into my head briefly. I wondered vaguely what she was up to tonight. Only it wasn't tonight. Heavens was years in the future. I shook off the thought. "Haven't found the time for that."

"You seem like that loner type," Ainsley said. "But I saw how Zigzag looked at you. I think she finds you attractive. But almost like you scare her a little too."

"I doubt she's scared. We've known each other a while."

"Like a prior hook-up?"

"Professionally. She used to be married to a synth girl so I think she's bi. Or tri. Whatever that is. She likes who she likes."

"I think she likes you."

I shrugged.

Ainsley pushed herself a little closer. "I think she's a crook. Seems like one."

"I know a lot of crooks."

"Like Amadeus? You two sure hate each other."

"Not hate. But he comes from a dangerous family. You spend enough time in a pit of vipers, you end up bit. I'd like to avoid it."

"He thinks you're dangerous too. I can tell."

"He can think what he wants."

"I think a man should be a little dangerous," she said and rested a hand on my arm. It sat there unmoving, but a sort of signal nonetheless.

She peered at me with her big brown eyes and edged a half an inch closer on her pillow. I contemplated the ceiling. After a moment her hand moved to my shoulder, and then she slid all the way over till her cheek was resting against it. She still smelled like cherry lip gloss, with an added freshness of shampoo.

"You think you would kill somebody if they broke this door down and came after us?"

"Someone with a gun? Probably. Unless they're faster."

"Would they be faster?"

"Coming through that door?" I studied it for a moment. "No."

She settled onto my shoulder again. "Good." She picked my arm up and put it over her so she could nestle into my chest. "You should come under the covers. It's harder to do this with you still on top."

"Do the best you can," I said.

If I ended up under those covers, I had little hope of coming back out again anytime soon.

As much as a romp in the sheets with Ainsley sounded like fun, taking advantage of her fear of being murdered somehow struck me as less-than-classy. A younger me wouldn't have cared, but for some reason it mattered to me tonight.

Ainsley had her arm draped across my abdomen now, her hand on my ribs. After a few minutes, it started edging south. When it reached the vicinity of my belt buckle, I grabbed her hand.

"You don't owe me anything, okay?"

Her eyes met mine.

"You can be here. Be safe. I'm not looking for anything from you in return."

"Okay. Sorry. It's just, some guys are like that."

When I didn't reply, she squeezed my hand, then curled herself into me a little tighter and closed her eyes.

I lay looking at the ceiling for a while.

Eventually my eyes started to droop.

A little sleep didn't sound like a bad idea.

But at that moment, the window lit up with a brilliant flash of blue. Ainsley and I both sat up and covered our eyes till the light faded.

Someone had activated the time gate. I slid off the bed and raised the blinds on the window. My room had a clear view of the driveway and the current location of the gate. Two men were standing in front of it. The tall one had on a black leather duster and dark glasses. The other wore a Cuban hat with a feather in the band and sported a bushy silver mustache.

Ainsley came over and wrapped her arm around mine.

The tall man looked up and glared at us through the window.

The agents from Time Crimes had arrived.

CHAPTER 13

Constantine Fallgrave was the best detective I'd ever heard of. I'd studied many of his cases and read each of his books. I'd never met him in person, however, so as I donned my boots to rejoin the others, I couldn't help the rush of adrenaline.

Ainsley Parker was making no special efforts on the famed detective's behalf, though she did pluck my hoodie from my overnight bag uninvited, and slipped it on. "Mind if I wear this? I'm cold."

She was no doubt cold due to the fact that she was barefoot and the yoga pants she'd put on were about the thickness of a water molecule. My hoodie was too large for her but she seemed to like not having the full use of her hands.

She padded after me as we walked into the hall. If she was at all concerned about the visual of coming out of my room wearing my clothes, she didn't show it.

We found the others on the landing of the main stairwell.

The tall, dark-haired agent had made it up the stairs and was talking to Winston Carlisle. Then came Fallgrave. He was a bit shorter than I expected, but carried the signature cane he was known for, a black rod of ash with a brass lion head on top. I'd heard stories of the cane. The underworld had too. They called it the yard stick, because anytime he was on a case, someone ended up doing time in the yard at Rookwood Penitentiary.

As far as I knew, no one had made up any stories like that about me.

Fallgrave leaned on the cane and surveyed the room with an appraising eye, his gaze finally alighting on me. The look was impenetrable. I took a step forward and extended my hand. "Inspector Fallgrave. It's a pleasure to meet you in person. I'm a follower of your work."

"A rare find. Have I arrested you?"

"Thankfully not. But I've read 'Body of Evidence' at least three times."

"Sounds as though you need a hobby. You're in the field?"

"Private detective," I said.

"Ah." His mustache twitched as he said it. He turned to his partner. "This is Agent Osborne."

Osborne only surveyed me in a cursory fashion, and when he addressed the group his tone was sharp. "We'll need everyone to give statements on what happened here tonight. Please prepare yourselves."

As he was speaking, Ainsley drew up beside me and slipped her arm around mine again. "Greyson has already done some investigating." Osborne fixated on her. Then he gave me a withering glare.

"Forgive us if we don't follow the lead of an amateur gumshoe."

Amateur? Ouch.

"Yet we will take all available information into account," Fallgrave added. "Regardless of the source." He aimed the point of his cane toward the drawing room. "Shall we?"

The drawing room had enough chairs for all of us, but when

Leo arrived, he chose to remain standing. Roman Amadeus had one leg crossed and was sipping a cup of coffee. If the investigation had him nervous at all, it didn't show. If anything, he looked bored.

Fallgrave kept his coat on as he positioned himself in the center of the room. "We will begin a formal investigation into the circumstances that occurred this evening and get statements from everyone, but I'd like to begin with the person who placed the call. I believe that was a Ms. Parker?"

Ainsley raised a hand from her place on the couch beside me.

"Walk with me into the adjoining room please. And tell me in your own words what you saw, if you would."

Ainsley swallowed and got off the sofa.

The pair adjourned to the salon, though the double doors stayed open. From my vantage point on the couch, they were still in view, but at a distance that made them difficult to hear.

Osborne conducted a similar interview, choosing Leo as his first victim. The pair made use of bar stools in the kitchen.

The rest of us were left to stare at one another as the process unfolded.

Mary Hurst stoked the fire in the hearth so we'd have more to look at.

After about fifteen minutes of questioning, Fallgrave and Ainsley returned and the agents repeated the operation with each of us. Waiting made me think of visits to the principal's office. Fallgrave spoke with Winston Carlisle, and Mary Hurst, then finally called for me.

I noted the voice recorder on the table when I sat down. No camera though.

"The others mentioned you took charge of the situation tonight," Fallgrave began. "Relying on police training, perhaps?"

"I did a linear academy but I've mostly learned by doing."

"Are you currently armed?"

"Gun is on my nightstand."

"Make and model?"

I told him.

"Agent Osborne and I are going to be collecting all firearms on the premises for safekeeping. Will that be a problem for you?"

I shifted in my seat and lied. "No problem."

"We did some preliminary research prior to arriving—background checks on each name we were provided on the transmission. It came to my attention that you aren't the only Greyson Travers."

It wasn't a question. I had the feeling he was expecting a response anyway. I didn't give one.

He checked his notes.

"You are, in fact, a duplicate, born of a paradoxical event in spacetime. Do you wish to share any information regarding how you came to depart your own timestream and take up residence in this one?"

"Not really."

Fallgrave made another note, then examined the tip of his pen. "You're here as an agent of Mrs. Rachel Rosen. Did she give you an indication as to why she didn't wish to attend herself?"

I thought about the photograph in my pocket, showing a version of me from the near future.

Rosen forcing me into the situation to avoid a paradox could be construed as blackmail by Time Crimes. But I wasn't here to rat on her.

"It's difficult terrain. Perhaps she didn't feel up to the exertion."

He scribbled some more. "This operation of acquiring a rare artifact from the past . . . you take this type of work often?"

"It's not my usual. I mostly work with linears. It's easier."

"Indeed. Using your secret skill of time travel to unravel the misdeeds of others must hold some attraction to you. However, I haven't found working for linears pays well. You have other sources of income?"

"Not at the moment."

He flipped a page on his pad. "Own any homes in this timestream?"

"No."

"Been to Attu before?"

"Never."

He twisted one tip of his mustache. "Can you tell me any reason why someone on this island would have wanted to harm your missing courier?"

"Stealing the Warsaw Pendulum seems the most obvious motive."

"Gaining the key to a secret treasure trove must even hold some allure for a man such as yourself."

"Less than you might think. Owning a lot of things has never been my style."

He leaned forward. "And what about the freedom such wealth could provide?"

I didn't have an argument for that.

Fallgrave checked his watch. When he looked up again, his expression was still inscrutable.

"I suspect I'll have many more questions for you come morning, Mr. Travers. But for now, why don't you retire. We'll be getting an early start."

"You don't want to hear my observations of what happened tonight?"

"In the morning. I suspect daylight will provide us with the clues we need to ask better questions."

I nodded and rose.

"And Mr. Travers, it would be best if each guest kept to their own quarters for the duration of the investigation. I'm not one to pry into private lives, but I've advised Ms. Parker that the grounds will be most safe with Agent Osborne and me here. And it does help us to know where to find everyone."

"Not a problem," I said.

At least that answer wasn't a lie.

Fallgrave was back to making notes as I left the room.

I had a distinct feeling I wouldn't like them.

CHAPTER 14

"I don't think Inspector Fallgrave knows I've solved murder cases before, Waldo."

I was back in my room, untying my boots.

"Perhaps you should inform him of your impeccable case record."

"I can't do that," I muttered. "It's supremely uncool. I'm not going to hand him a list of my accomplishments and wait for him to be impressed."

"You'd like to have his respect without having to inform him of what you've achieved."

"A little professional courtesy would be nice. But having to tell people something like that just cheapens it."

"Hmm. Like posting shirtless pictures on online dating profiles," Waldo said. "Displaying a fit body for other humans is something that is only attractive if it happens organically."

"Weird analogy, man. Why have you been researching online dating profiles?"

"Since our last case, I'm endeavoring to better understand human connection. So far, I have yet to encounter a comprehensive resource."

"I doubt you'll find it in the online dating scene."

"Observing your behavior with dates has been very informative."

"Tonight was not a date."

"And yet witnessing a traumatic event together seemed to bring you and Miss Parker closer together. Perhaps persons seeking connection should attend more traumatic events."

"If you ever start a dating service, remind me to steer clear."

"Have you formulated any theories about what happened tonight?"

I set my boots in the corner, then dropped to the carpet near the bed for some push-ups. "The way things went down makes it difficult. But Fallgrave was right. Morning will bring more clarity."

I pumped out a set of fifty reps and sat back on my knees to regain my breath.

"The manner in which you were interviewed did not seem standard procedure," Waldo said. "Do you feel Inspector Fallgrave will make use of your professional experience? He seemed more intent on your past."

"Running background checks is standard. And I doubt he needs my help."

"Yet you were here while the event unfolded. Fallgrave was not. It gives you an advantage as an investigator."

"It's not a competition, Waldo. Whoever did the shooting tonight will have made mistakes. An inspector like Fallgrave will be methodical and thorough. I've studied his methods. He'll run them down."

"You don't intend to assist?"

"He doesn't need me interfering. If he asks for help, I'll give it."

"And what of Agent Osborne? Do you also rate his detective skills above your own?"

"Osborne has been Fallgrave's partner for years. I'm sure he has his uses. But Fallgrave's the brains to that duo. And I'm not letting you lure me into making comparisons. Nobody hands out awards for Best Detective."

"Osborne is Fallgrave's Watson," Waldo said. "Do you ever wish that you had a partner like that?"

"I have you, Waldo," I said as I started another set of push-ups. "You're better than ten Osbornes. That's a comparison I'll give you."

"It is nice to be appreciated, but it's a pity about the lack of awards. I think my name would look excellent engraved on a plaque for posterity."

I paused my push-ups and held up one empty palm. "I made this statue in your likeness instead. You like it?"

"Ha. Ha. You're hilarious."

I smirked and kept going.

I was getting out of the shower fifteen minutes later when the fatigue caught up to me. I mopped off with a towel and stared at the mirror. I was a man with plenty of years ahead of me. Maybe the victim had been too. They were cashed out now, though. Was I in danger of being next? I found it unlikely, but a nagging feeling in my gut wouldn't unknot itself. Maybe I should be more careful on this island.

Someone knocked on the door.

I tightened the towel around my waist and scooped my Stinger off the dresser before making my way to the door.

"Who is it?"

"Agent Osborne. Here for that pistol of yours."

I frowned and looked down at my gun. The thought of handing over my only weapon pained me.

"Hang on a minute."

Osborne knocked again.

"Just got out of the shower," I explained to the door.

"I haven't got all night."

There was no excuse I could think of that would satisfy him. I opened the hallway door with a sigh.

Osborne surveyed me. "It's late. I recommend you stay in your room the rest of the night."

"Worried I'll go streaking in the halls?"

He held out his hand for my gun.

"Where will this be if I need it?" I asked.

"In my possession."

"Comforting." I turned the pistol around and handed it to him grip-first. "You get Leo and Roman's guns too?"

"I did." He looked mine over. "Palm print sensor?"

"Among other things. Assures the bullets are flying the right direction."

"You'll be texted a receipt whenever we get reception again."

"I'll hold my breath."

"Any other firearms in your possession?"

"Nope."

"We'll be conducting a detailed search of the premises tomorrow. If it is found that you are lying it will be considered as obstructing an investigation and you'll be arrested."

"You have my only gun. Scouts honor."

He gave a curt nod and walked back through the library. Charming guy.

I still had the towel on, but I felt naked.

My eyes drifted to the painting on the far library wall that disguised the safe and the current location of my chronometer.

If any bad guys needed a comeuppance tonight, they were going to have to settle for my fists.

I closed my door. I had only just located a clean shirt in my bag when I had another knock. What else of mine could Osborne want? He wasn't getting the towel. I stormed back and flung the door open.

Ainsley Parker breezed in.

"That guy took *forever* doing his rounds. Doesn't he know we need sleep?" She dumped her bag on the dresser next to mine.

"Welcome back. Not much for rule following, I see."

Ainsley rolled her eyes. "They think they can get me all alone but I'm not falling for it. That's just what the killer wants."

I sighed and shut the door. The clock on the wall showed it was almost two. Probably too cold for me to throw her out a window.

Ainsley stripped out of my sweatshirt and tossed it over my bag.

"Do you snore?"

"Like a freight train. You might not hear it from your room."

She cocked a hand on her hip.

"I'm joking. You're welcome to stay."

She plucked some earplugs and an eye mask from her bag, then marched over to the bed, promptly climbing in. She put in her earplugs, then burrowed under the covers until I could barely see her.

I dressed in workout pants and a T-shirt, then pulled back the covers on my side of the bed.

Then came another knock at the door.

Good God. What now?

I opened the door to find Zhang Zi glowering at me.

"What can I do for you, Zigzag? Don't tell me you're scared of the dark too."

"What? No. We need to talk."

I waved her in. Maybe I should install a revolving door.

When she came in, Zigzag was hugging her elbows and glaring. Was a lot of that going around tonight.

"You going to explain?"

I frowned. "Explain what?"

"I saw what you did."

"Enlighten me."

She scrutinized me intently. "I thought you had a code. Protect the innocent. Avoid paradoxes. All that shit. Was that just for show or something?"

"You're not making any sense."

"I saw you. In the fog."

"And I saw you. What of it?"

She tightened her jaw and shook her head.

"If you have something to say, spit it out. What did you see tonight?"

Her mouth opened, but she hesitated. "Your face is . . ."

"What is *she* doing here?" Ainsley sat up in the bed and pulled out an earplug.

Zigzag whipped around in surprise. "What the fuck?"

I gestured toward the bed. "This one has developed a bit of an aversion to her room."

"It's called safety in numbers," Ainsley said. "And he's the only one I can trust."

Zigzag fixed me with another glare, then stormed out into the dark again. Apparently she didn't share the sentiment.

I walked to the door and peeked my head into the library. "Anyone else?"

The library was mercifully vacant.

The lock made a satisfying click when I turned it.

Ainsley was already back under the covers.

I stared at the lump she made. Dad probably would have slept on the floor like a gentleman.

The hell if I was going to.

I crawled into my side of the bed and put an extra pillow over my head for good measure.

I slept like the dead.

CHAPTER 15

I woke to find Ainsley Parker asleep on my chest and strands of her auburn hair in my mouth.

Out the window, sunlight was making a feeble attempt to breach the horizon.

Extricating myself from Ainsley's grasp took a bit of doing, but I managed to not wake her. I dressed and slipped out quietly, locking the door behind me.

I was crossing the library when the voice accosted me.

"Good to find you awake."

Constantine Fallgrave was seated in one of the armchairs facing the windows. He set a coffee mug down on the table beside him. "I'd like your assistance this morning if you'd care to give it." He looked like he had already dressed for the outdoors.

I gestured to the coffee mug. "Any more where that came from?"

"Have Ms. Hurst put yours in a travel mug. We have a lot of ground to cover."

I found Mary Hurst in the kitchen prepping for a meal. She gave me a wary nod as a greeting. She looked displeased about something but wasn't chatty.

Her coffee was good. I snagged a croissant on the way out too, but had to wait on whatever else she was fixing.

Fallgrave was waiting for me by the main door, his mustache looking bushier than ever. Osborne appeared from the side corridor, dressed in a black trench coat. He reminded me of what Dracula would look like as a cop.

"Agent Osborne is going to keep an eye on the other guests while you and I talk," Fallgrave said. "Shall we get to work?" He gestured to the door with his cane.

The morning air was cool but the fog from the previous night had dissipated enough for the sky to be visible. A gray ocean horizon was in view as well. Patches of mist still clung to the island but the rising sun was slowly making its presence felt.

Fallgrave took his time descending the stairs. I sipped my coffee until he reached the ground level.

The inspector scrutinized the sparse landscape as he buttoned his coat. "Now, Mr. Travers, if you would be so kind, please take me through your recollection of last night's events."

I put on my shades and activated the Breadcrumbs app again. We walked.

In daylight, it seemed a shorter distance to the original site of the time gate, even with the inspector limping. Fallgrave snapped pictures as we walked, noting the crushed grass in various locations. I sipped more coffee and let Waldo do my recording via the cameras in my shades.

"This is where I last saw Leo," I said, noting a departure from the main path that cut across the hillside.

Fallgrave made a note.

The spot the truck had been still showed evidence of the previous night's search. We followed Winston Carlisle's path down the hill and back up again. Mine and Ainsley's path to the second site of the gate was clearly visible too. Fallgrave's camera clicked with each new location.

With the help of the Breadcrumbs app, I was able to retrace my original route with precision, including where I'd heard the gunshots. My flashlight lay on the ground there and was still on, though the bulb had dimmed. I picked it up and switched it off once Fallgrave had his photo.

"It seems we have many questions to resolve," he said, surveying the grassy hillside.

"It'll be a tough spot to jump back in time to witness," I said. "The fog and the general confusion will complicate things. High grass and bad weather make for a shit landing sight. Might be able to precede the events and install a few hidden cameras. But if they are here, we don't really want to go looking for them now."

"You have a reputation as a man mindful of paradoxes," Fallgrave said as we continued through the grass.

"Hard to solve the case if we accidentally split the timeline by changing the events."

"You've no doubt considered the temporal issues we face with the identity of our shooter."

"I see several. Especially because it's possible no one *is* our shooter yet."

Fallgrave nodded. "I've been pondering the same problem. Discerning a motive for the shooting presents a question of tenses. Not only who might have wanted to shoot Logan Tyler, but also who might yet decide to come back and shoot Logan Tyler from the future."

It was a problem you only had to consider when dealing with time travelers as suspects. But we had six on this island at the time of the shooting, not including the presumed victim. It was possible none were the shooter now, but one would be soon.

It's hard to catch a killer who isn't one yet.

"Shooter could also still be an outsider," Fallgrave observed.

It was possible. But in my mind, unlikely. I had a feeling he thought so too.

"No one on this island has shared that they knew this Logan Tyler person by sight," Fallgrave continued. "Nor has anyone expressed a desire to eliminate the courier. Though it would seem we certainly have a motive available for anyone to do so. Our list of suspects is not small."

We walked on and arrived at the location of the shooting.

The color of the blood on the grass had darkened overnight but was still clearly visible. It almost looked like there was more of it than when I'd observed the scene last night. Fallgrave pushed at some of the stems with the foot of his cane. "Let's play a game, Mr. Travers. Let us pretend you were the shooter. How would you have done it?"

My coffee cup was empty. I toyed with it as I ran the events though my mind. "A shooter would have to find a time to jump in, possibly using the same time gate as the victim."

"Or use a chronometer such as the ones currently in the wall safe," Fallgrave added.

"Possibly. One way or another, if the shooter was me, I still would've needed time away from the others to make a jump."

"Easy to do with the chronometer you wore last night. Less easy with a gate."

"Sure. Gate was a long walk away from the lodge last night," I admitted. "But it's close now."

Fallgrave looked back up the hill toward the lodge.

"Agent Osborne and I ensured the gate was sufficiently locked after our arrival," Fallgrave said. "And someone had already done that work for us. It's impossible for someone to use it currently, even if we let them get close."

"So presuming the shooter wasn't someone else already lying in wait, it would need to be a chronometer," I said. "Or someone using the gate from a different time when it isn't locked. They'd have to have moved the truck and the time gate after they got here so that this Logan Tyler would have arrived somewhere other than expected."

"A place where Ms. Hurst couldn't have located the arrival," Fallgrave said.

"So the gate activates. Logan Tyler shows up. Likely disoriented. Wanders uphill a ways, headed toward the lodge. Shooter does some shooting. Two shots for good measure. Then they moved the body for some reason."

"Dragged it a good distance it seems." Fallgrave gestured with his cane to the streaks of blood in the crushed grass. "And then?"

"Then made it disappear," I said.

"To when, we wonder." Fallgrave's mustache twitched. "Or the body could still be hidden on the island."

"No vehicle tracks," I countered. "Would have needed the ATV or something equivalent. Only one we heard last night was being ridden by Mary Hurst and she had Leo aboard. They would have noticed if it had been covered in blood."

"So the most likely suspects remain someone with a chronometer who jumped in and out quickly," Fallgrave said. "Possibly taking the body with them."

"Let's not forget there were two chronometers worn last night," I said.

"Indeed," Fallgrave replied. "I think it's time I had another conversation with Roman Amadeus."

CHAPTER 16

Winston Carlisle was studying a topographical map of the island mounted to a wall of the drawing room when we got back. He had on a tweed vest today, making him look especially old fashioned. There was an air of nostalgia to the man that I enjoyed, whether he was aware of it or not.

He noted me entering the room and nodded as I approached.

"I understand you were able to walk the scene from last night with the inspector," he said. "Is he enlisting your aid in the investigation?"

"Maybe."

I still wasn't sure whether my walk with Fallgrave had been meant to help him or to clarify where I stood on his list of suspects.

"Can't say I'd have the stomach for your business," Carlisle said. "Did you find a body?"

I shook my head.

He looked relieved.

"Have a question I need to ask you, Winston. Last night as I was walking around on the deck, I saw a light out to the northwest. I think it might have been on the shore of the inlet out there. Any idea what it might have been?"

"Northwest, you say? No. Nothing that way. Everything interesting on this island came inland from the east, back past the peace monument and by way of the old airfield."

"What about a boat?"

"I suppose it's possible, but I can't imagine much being out this far without us hearing it. I keep a scanner in my room that would pick up any VHF radio communications. In that fog last night, you would have a hard time seeing that far anyway. Are you sure you saw a light?"

"Not betting my life on it. I was pretty tired at the time, but I saw something." I consulted the map on the wall. "How far out is this point here?"

"Mile and a half perhaps."

I traced my finger back along the shore toward our location. "Hard terrain?"

"Not for an athletic person like yourself."

I studied the map some more, but had no epiphanies. Winston gestured toward the dining room. "Ms. Hurst has informed me that breakfast and lunch have been combined into a brunch this morning on account of some kind of shortage. Shall we investigate?"

"Why not." I followed him to the dining room.

Mary had laid out the food as a buffet and it appeared several guests had already eaten. Mary was cleaning up dirty dishes on one end of the long dining table.

"I understand we're not to expect another meal until suppertime, Mary?" Winston inquired.

"Won't be fancy either," she replied. "Especially if any more thievery is encountered."

I noted her sour expression. "Someone stole food?"

"An entire pie I'd defrosted last night, plus a bottle of champagne meant for mimosas. And a bowl of hard boiled eggs.

Pan of brownies I baked is gone too. Went to bed a bit after midnight last night. It was there. This morning it wasn't."

Brownies were missing? That was definitely a crime.

"Why steal food when it's all paid for anyway?" I asked.

Mary shrugged. "Don't ask me. I just work here. I have another bottle of champagne so it's not the end of the world, but I don't appreciate having to make plans for a meal twice."

I turned to Winston. "Might be worth asking if anyone else had anything go missing in the night."

"You think the food thief has something to do with the shooting incident?"

"Don't know what I think. Just figured we can ask."

He agreed.

Someone stealing food didn't make a lot of sense in this group. We had plenty at dinner even if it was cut short. Maybe Leo was trying to keep his calorie count up to maintain muscle mass. He looked like a bodybuilder. Eggs would make sense. But a whole pan of brownies?

Brunch looked good. I helped myself to roasted garlic potatoes and fruit with what looked to be some sort of plant-based sausage. The coffee was still fresh too. By the time Winston and I had made our way through the buffet options, Inspector Fallgrave and Osborne had rallied the other guests. Roman and Leo looked none-too-pleased to be in attendance. Zigzag was still grumpy as well. She wasn't making eye contact with me. Whatever it was she had wanted to accuse me of last night must not have been pressing enough to discuss in public. I figured she'd get around to spitting it out eventually.

Everyone took seats around the long table.

Ainsley Parker was the last member of the group to wander in. She'd found time to fix her hair and makeup but was still in the leggings she'd slept in. She strode over and pulled out a chair next to me but immediately crossed her arms when she'd sat.

"You should have told me you were leaving this morning," she whispered. "Someone could have murdered me while you were out."

"Glad you survived."

"You're gonna feel bad if I die and you don't save me."

I rested my elbows on the table and folded my hands. "Anyone have a good reason to kill you?"

"Killers don't need reasons. Don't you watch the news?"

She had a point, but I had a hard time believing this was going to be one of those cases. If someone in this lodge had killed Logan Tyler, I figured they had a very good reason.

Fallgrave cleared his throat. "Agent Osborne has brought to my attention that sometime last night, the tachyon pulse transmitter used to call us here was disabled. It would appear someone is attempting to cut off communications with other times. As such, we have been unable to request additional agents for this investigation."

That was news.

"Anyone have any information to share on the subject?" Osborne added.

A few glances were made around the room.

"She was out of her room last night," Ainsley said, pointing to Zigzag.

Zigzag scowled, but didn't reply.

"Is that true?" Osborne asked.

"I didn't go anywhere near the TPT," she snapped.

"And just where *did* you go?" Osborne pulled an electronic pad from his pocket to make a note.

"She came to see me," I said. "A little past two."

"After I'd specifically instructed all of you to stay in your rooms," Osborne said. His gaze found Ainsley as well.

I was sensing he was a bit of a stickler for the rules.

"We had a brief chat and she left," I said.

"What did you and Miss Zhang discuss?" Agent Fallgrave asked.

"Bit confused about that myself."

Fallgrave looked at Zigzag but it was clear she wasn't open to sharing.

"The situation on this island is quite serious," Fallgrave said, shifting his grip on his cane. "Thanks to this saboteur last night, we are now cut off from communication. It is my intention to return to the scene of the crime via the time gate at the earliest opportunity and resolve who the culprit is. But until then, it is of the utmost importance that each and every one of you cooperate to ensure your ongoing safety for the next twenty-four hours."

"You think the killer is still on this island," Ainsley said.

"I am convinced of it," Fallgrave said. "And they are as trapped as we are. Trapped things are very dangerous, Ms. Parker."

Ainsley shrank a little closer to me.

"But let me assure you," Fallgrave waved his cane, "whenever and wherever this killer goes, there is no escape from a relentless application of logic and reason. Therefore, there is no escape from me."

CHAPTER 17

The way I saw it, the case was in good hands. Fallgrave and Osborne had decided to conduct another interview with Roman Amadeus and his gun thug in the salon after brunch. The rest of us had been cut loose.

Suited me fine. But while I retrieved my loaner coat from the hall closet, I had a shadow.

Ainsley Parker was sticking to me like gum on a shoe. She certainly wasn't hard to look at, so I'd had worse company.

"Where are you going?" she asked.

"Out."

"Is that smart?"

I shrugged. "I wanna check on something."

"Shouldn't we all stay together for safety?"

"The killer is probably in this lodge. So are all the guns. As far as places to get shot goes, this might be the best choice."

She glanced back toward the drawing room where Zigzag and Winston Carlisle were commiserating over coffee. The look Zigzag gave Ainsley may as well have been a dagger.

Ainsley said, "I'll get my jacket."

The sky was back to overcast, but it was a thin layer. Still cold but no rain yet. That was a mercy. I donned my sunglasses and tapped my earpiece.

"Waldo, I want to plot a course northwest. Let's map as we go."

"You wish to search for the source of the light you saw last night?"

"Call me curious."

"I can approximate a location based on your position on the porch and what would have been visible."

"Nice. Let's see what we can find."

The terrain was sparse but challenging to navigate due to the high grasses and slopes. Ainsley and I forged northwest along the island with the mountains to our left and the inlet to our right. We occasionally lost sight of the lodge going through gullies, but regained it again whenever we neared the shore.

Some spindly cranes watched us pass but didn't fly off.

I was struck again by the barren strangeness of the place. Not a single tree to be seen, just mile after mile of volcanic rock and boggy scrub. The tips of the mountains still had snow. Probably would've been heaven for a goat. It was a lonely place for humans. The only bit of cheer was the occasional cluster of wildflowers eking an existence amongst the grass stems. A few small, yellow, spring blooms dotted the green.

"You think anyone has ever been out this way before?" Ainsley asked. "It's so far from anything."

"We aren't the first." I observed the grass and mud. Then I pointed. "That's a footprint."

Ainsley stepped closer to where I was indicating and noted the imprint of a boot in the soft earth.

"From last night?"

"Not sure. But it hasn't dried out. I'd guess sometime in the last twenty-four hours."

Ainsley eyed the landscape with a new caution. "What if they have a gun?"

"Let's hope they don't."

I put a boot print in the ground near the one I'd found. Mine was larger. Didn't narrow it down much, but it was something.

There was more evidence the farther we walked. Broken grass stems. More bootprints. Then we saw the wreck.

I noted the tail first. It was sun-bleached and covered in bird shit, but still recognizable as a plane. I didn't know too much about makes and models but I recognized the canopy frame and rounded engine cowling as WWII era. The faded red paint on one crumpled wing gave away that it had once been Japanese. It had also once been a floatplane, but the boggy ground had completely swallowed the central pontoon. Another smaller wing pontoon looked like it had been sheared off or cannibalized. Only its mount remained.

We approached cautiously. There were more bootprints in the grass. Mud on the right wing. There was no sign of anyone now though. I climbed up to have a better look. The canopy of the plane had been forced open, and recently. The interior of the plane smelled old and musty, but it was relatively clean considering the state of the wreck. And still dry. The canopy windows were crusted with dirt and bird droppings but none had gotten inside the cockpit. This plane had probably been here for eighty years. I was surprised anyone had even managed to pry it open. But someone had. And judging by the fresh dirt and the state of one yellow flower petal that had hitched a ride, it had been in the last day. The flower petal was still bright.

"What were they doing out here?" Ainsley said.

I surveyed the cockpit. It was cramped but not the worst place in the world to be if you needed somewhere dry for the night. Unless there had been another reason. Could there have been something of value in the plane?

My flashlight was so dim that it wasn't much use, but I searched anyway. A detailed inspection might come up with some fingerprints, but none jumped out at me. Even Waldo couldn't detect any. Maybe whoever had come out here had worn gloves. Could someone have hidden something out here?

I donned my gloves and felt around under the seats.

There was an old oxygen canister and some deteriorated seat stuffing but no Warsaw Pendulum.

Then my fingers hit something hard that clunked. I pulled it out and discovered it was a tire iron. I didn't know a lot about float planes, but I knew they didn't need tire changes. The tip of the tire iron showed flecks of paint that matched the scuffs around the canopy latch. Explained how they forced their way in.

I closed the canopy and kept the tire iron.

This was a definite mystery. Had someone walked all the way out here last night? Zigzag maybe? Why?

When I stood up I could just make out the distant lodge. With the wind shifting the fog last night it was possible the light I saw could have come from right here. Likely even.

What the hell were they doing out here so late?

"Is there anyone else who could have known we'd be on this island?" I asked.

Ainsley shrugged. "No one. Everyone involved in the project is here. Except your employer."

"And Weintraub."

"Oh. Right. Him too."

"You were hired by Weintraub. You ever meet him?"

She pushed her hands farther into the pockets of her pink puffy jacket. "I'm an employee of the club, so it's Winston that I officially work for. Weintraub hired Winston. I never met him."

"You have any guesses on why Weintraub isn't here? This whole thing was his operation."

She shook her head. "I don't know. I just ran risk analysis to greenlight the project."

Something wasn't adding up. If I had gone to the effort of planning this job, I would have wanted to see it through. Why do all this setup and skip the good part when the key to the treasure was due to show up? I stared at the distant lodge some more.

"Attu island is a long way from Warsaw, but it's all from the same era. Is there any way the courier could have planned their route through here before arriving by time gate?"

"Couriers sometimes transfer gates a few times on the way, but this one didn't. The trip was straight to Attu."

"Who selected this Logan Tyler as the courier?"

"Weintraub picked everyone on the job. Courier too."

"You ever meet Tyler?"

She shook her head.

I didn't like that this group was missing two of its key players. Logan Tyler was almost certainly dead, but we still didn't have a body to prove it.

"When you saw someone get shot last night, was it two men?"

"It was hard to see, but I think so. The one shooting for sure."

"Two shots?"

She nodded, then looked to the lodge. "Can we go back? I don't like it out here. It's eerie."

I scanned the barren landscape once more. She wasn't wrong. The quiet was almost too calm. Like it was hiding something.

And I was missing it.

"Okay, let's go."

We walked back. I only turned around once to look at the plane.

If it held a secret, it was doing a good job of keeping it.

CHAPTER 18

"This case will be solved through persistent application of logic and reason. Not gut feelings," Fallgrave said. He had received my report on the floatplane with mild interest but little more. He was seated in the salon where he had set up a temporary office and I stood before him. "Agent Osborne will check the tire iron for prints and investigate the site. But if you intend to conduct more searches for the Warsaw Pendulum, I would suggest you run the plans by me first."

"Figured you wanted all the information you can get," I said.

"If it is derived from diligent detective work, yes. But you may omit your *intuitions* on the matter. Your gut feelings do not interest me." He palmed the lion head topper on his cane, rubbing it absentmindedly. "The difference between a great detective and a middling one primarily comes here." He tapped a finger to his temple. "Solely relying on logic, Mr. Travers. Anything else muddies the waters and gives the advantage to our enemy."

"How about good old-fashioned poking around till something wiggles?"

Fallgrave didn't smile. Or if he did, his mustache hid all signs. His eyes certainly didn't. "That will be all for now, Mr. Travers."

I guess that was all.

I meandered back to the drawing room. Ainsley had seen fit to unglue herself from me and find a bathroom. I was sure she'd be back soon enough. Maybe she had a dress made of cling wrap to model for me. But I used the respite to head back toward the library.

"Your mentor seemed displeased with your assistance," Waldo said in my ear.

"No one is displeased with me, Waldo. I'm delightful."

"You certainly believe yourself to be."

"Fallgrave is going to conduct his investigation his way. He's probably right. Doesn't bother me."

"And yet it would not be how *you* would conduct the investigation."

"True. My way would involve more punching of people to see what they know. Mostly Roman."

"The inspector called you 'middling.'"

"I'm sure he meant it as a compliment."

"There are many things I still don't understand about your dealings with other humans. Do you ever admit that some people just don't like you?"

"The presumption that I should care becomes a factor."

"Yet you do care."

"I respect myself, Waldo. And you like me. What more could a man want?"

"What about Miss Archer?"

That gave me pause. Thoughts of Heavens had been doing that lately. "Sure. Heavens' opinion matters."

"So only the opinions of people you respect matter?"

"I respect Fallgrave professionally. He's excellent at what he does. Whether or not he likes me personally doesn't change that."

"Your detachment seems useful. Perhaps it shields you from emotional pain."

"That's actually what bourbon is for. When did this become Analyze Greyson Day?"

"I analyze everyone. But you require more of it."

"I'll take that as a compliment too."

"You would."

I made it to the library.

Winston Carlisle was standing over a table at one side of the room viewing a cluster of what appeared to be tiny toy soldiers he had laid out. It was a diorama. The island.

He heard my approach and turned.

"Planning an attack?" I asked.

He tucked his hands into his blazer pockets. "A bit of a lost cause now. I had intended to fill some of the wait time till the gate reopened with a brief presentation I'd prepared."

I smiled. How like a historian to believe that his guests would have wanted to listen to a history lecture in their free time.

"What was the gist of the presentation?"

"The story of the war. This island's part in it. This was the only place where the United States conducted a ground battle on US soil during World War II. A fascinating tale when you learn about some of the people involved."

"Don't think I'd ever even heard of Attu before coming here."

"Most haven't. So many other battles throughout the war have provided more fodder for film and television, but this spot had its relevance. It's a shame they only teach the history with the most Hollywood appeal anymore."

His presentation looked like something from a past century. He might have made the figurines himself. He picked up one figurine modeling a heavy coat with the rising sun on its sleeve. "The Japanese had a foothold on US soil. Albeit briefly. They were a brave and determined enemy. Passionate. Hard to kill. They had over twenty-three hundred soldiers. All but twenty-eight of them died here."

I looked out the windows to the desolate hills. "Not an easy place to fight."

"Exposure was the most dangerous threat. On Attu you fight the weather first and each other second."

I told him about the floatplane I'd found.

"Likely a Mitsubishi A6M. You may have heard it called a Zero. The Japanese had a floatplane version."

"Nothing to do with Nazi Germany and our Warsaw Pendulum though."

"Can't imagine a connection. Other than we are all on the same island now."

"You think the pendulum is still here?"

He looked pensive. "I feel very certain that the agent we hired was a reliable one. The route we charted through time was also good. There is no reason to suspect that anything would have impeded their arrival. Not until last night anyway."

"If the pendulum is here, someone is doing a good job of hiding it."

"Indeed."

"What else can you tell me about Roman Amadeus's involvement?"

"Only what we've already discussed. He provided the time gates, and the relocation equipment. And of course he was instrumental in the construction of this lodge. But that's the extent of it."

"Did he know the route times? Locations?"

"No. That was confidential."

"But he knew valuables were being transferred. And generally from when."

"Anyone with even a passing interest in Warsaw could know about the cache from the ghetto. And our team had the basic knowledge for the assignment."

"You don't find it at all odd that he wanted to participate in this? A historical preservation mission?"

"You think he might have an ulterior motive?"

"No. I'm positive he has an ulterior motive, but I don't know what it is yet. He gave me the impression there may be something else besides the Warsaw cache in that shipment."

"You don't trust Mr. Amadeus."

"I don't trust anyone on this island."

To his credit, Winston didn't look offended.

"Judging by our experience thus far, that may prove a beneficial strategy," he admitted. He looked over the diorama of little plastic soldiers, then reached out with an index finger and toppled one.

The remaining plastic soldiers didn't look nervous. But maybe they ought to be.

CHAPTER 19

The tachyon pulse transmitter wasn't broken.

It sure wasn't going to work anytime soon, though.

I was studying the device in the hallway when a shadow on the floor grew from my left. Leo was blocking the light from the drawing room doorway with all his compact, muscle bound glory.

"Planning to wreck that thing some more?" he asked.

I frowned at him, then went back to looking at the TPT. "It's not wrecked. It has parts missing. It's different. Means whoever disabled it didn't want to take it out of service permanently."

"It was around long enough for you to call the cops."

It had been Ainsley who called the cops, but I didn't bother to correct him. "That bother you for some reason?" I rotated the TPT on the table and observed the open back. The power supply was still there but the transmission encoder was gone. So was the temporal frequency oscillator.

"You're trying to get my boss in trouble," Leo said.

"If he didn't do anything wrong, then he's got nothing to worry about. Unless you know something he might get in trouble for."

"I think you should butt out of it."

He'd gotten a little closer. I could detect his cologne. Smelled like he'd wiped some free samples from a men's fitness magazine all over himself.

I turned to face him.

"Someone got shot out there last night, Leo. Police were always going to get involved."

"Don't see 'em sitting *you* in a room for hours asking questions."

"Maybe that's because I'm not a hired gun for a known gangster."

"Don't need a gun to deal with you." He flexed his neck as he said it. Maybe he planned to nuzzle me into submission.

"I admire your loyalty to your boss, Leo. But if Roman murdered someone last night, I'm not going to let that slide."

"You aren't the cops."

"But I was hired to retrieve the Warsaw Pendulum. If Roman has it, then that's who I'm going to take it from. And if he goes down for murder as a result, that's his fault."

"Seems to me this whole thing is a goddamn setup. You just want to pin something on us to cut us out of the deal."

"You a big collector of mid-twentieth-century, Jewish artifacts, Leo?"

He narrowed his eyes.

"Or is there something else in that shipment that interests you and your boss?"

Leo just kept glaring at me. He flexed some more.

I checked out his feet. They were smaller than mine. "You happen to go for a walk with a crowbar last night?"

He scrunched up his face. "Whatchu talkin about?"

"Visit any old war planes?"

He looked genuinely confused. He also looked like he was weighing the benefits of using me as a punching bag. There wouldn't be many.

He must have decided the same thing because he gave a little snort and backed away a step. "You best butt the hell out of all this if you know what's good for you. I'm warning you."

I was going to do no such thing, but I didn't feel now was the best time to burst his bubble.

The moment he was gone, Ainsley Parker appeared in the doorway. She was getting really good at it. She cast a quick glance the way Leo had gone. "What was that about?"

"He's mad I won't snuggle by the fire with him."

Ainsley had changed. She'd braided her hair and now wore a cozy knit sweater with blue jeans that had clearly been applied with a vacuum sealer. Whatever she did for exercise was working for her. Being a young twenty-something likely didn't hurt.

Her eyes fell on the TPT. "Are you trying to make that work?"

"It's beyond help for the moment."

"Bummer. So what do we do now?"

I checked the time. It was another eight hours till the time gate opened. And seven hours and fifty-five minutes till the safe with my chronometer inside would unlock.

Seemed like a good time for a snack. I'd think of a better plan on a full stomach.

Mary Hurst was in the kitchen, already prepping for dinner.

She eyed us warily when we walked in. "If you two come sniffing around for lunch we ain't got it. Dinner is in five hours. But there's a few things over there you can help yourselves to." She gestured with a chopping knife to a basket full of fruit and the box of pastries.

I wandered over to investigate.

"You doing okay?" Ainsley asked. "You need any help?"

Mary harrumphed slightly. "I'm fine." She continued chopping. "Though I still don't understand how a bunch of time travelers aren't better at cleaning up their own messes. Why don't you all just go back and stop this nonsense from happening to begin with? We could be having a normal day right now."

"Time doesn't work that way," Ainsley said. "You can't change the past. If you do, you might create a split future."

"So you can fix it, but you won't? Sounds like a cop out."

Ainsley looked to me for help.

"It's harder than you think," I explained. "If we go back and observe without changing events, that may be fine, but if we alter the past, it creates a paradox that could divert the future. It's messy. You likely wouldn't notice. Your timeline would continue unaltered, but whoever went back and made the change might find themselves living in an alternate reality. Still wouldn't fix things here."

Mary put her knife aside and tossed the chopped vegetables into a pot. "We had a guest arrive last night and now that guest is probably dead. If I could do what you could do, I wouldn't be waiting around for Mr. Mustache to do all the work. Pretty sure I'd have this killer nabbed by now."

I rubbed an apple on my shirt, then took a bite. She might be right. A time traveling Mary Hurst would be a force to be reckoned with. But we were right too. Time travel was complicated. The last thing in the world we needed was someone going off half-cocked and duplicating the timestream.

"Whoever shot Logan Tyler is probably still on this island," I said. "And we have Fallgrave now."

"Until someone unlocks that gate of yours again," Mary countered. "Then your killer flies the coop."

She was serving more hot truth. We had one afternoon and evening when we could be sure the pendulum thief was nearby. Once people started leaving the island, the odds of nailing the killer dropped to near zero. I had confidence in Fallgrave's methods, but maybe I was being too lax in my approach. It was still a short window of time, even for a detective of his caliber. More poking around might be warranted.

While Ainsley and Mary continued their discussion of who they thought the shooter could be, I slipped the photo Rosen had given me from my pocket. My future self still stared out at the sparse Attu landscape.

I wasn't used to being short on time during a case, but this might be the one I'd have to worry about. If I didn't have a grip on who the pendulum thief was in the next eight hours, I could be facing a paradox of my own making. I finished my apple and tossed the core in the trash, then pocketed the photo again.

"All right, Ainsley. Let's go."

We had a killer to find.

CHAPTER 20

"I think this is crazy," Ainsley whispered.

"Don't worry. I do it all the time." I had my lock pick in the doorknob of Roman's room and in a matter of ten seconds I had it open. I pushed the door wide and gestured to Ainsley. "Ladies first?"

"No!" she hissed. "What if he shows up?"

I'd done a quick search for Roman and Leo prior to attempting this stunt and noted them lighting cigars on the porch. I figured I had a good twenty minutes for poking around.

"Keep a lookout then."

Roman's room was even tidier than I expected. The bed was made with tight corners, clothing hung neatly in the closet. I opened a few drawers and even his designer socks were carefully folded. And arranged by color. I poked around the bathroom briefly. His cologne didn't look like it came from a fitness magazine.

There weren't a lot of places to hide things. I checked under the bed, lifted the pillows. I even searched his shoes. His suitcase was a challenge. I lifted each item out carefully, noting the order so I'd have a way to put it back neatly. More designer clothes. A hardcover copy of "A Gentleman in Moscow." At least he read. Doubted I'd find that in Leo's bag.

There were no neatly-typed and signed murder confessions.

I felt around the liner of the bag. Near one roller wheel attachment, I found a lump under the fabric. Huh. Attaching hardware? The lump didn't exist on the other side. Very curious.

I felt around some more. I pushed at the lump. It moved. I pushed a little more and it moved all the way to the seam and poked out a little from an incision there. It was tough to get a grip on it wearing my gloves but I finally managed it. It was a data drive. An itty bitty one.

Fun. I slipped it into my pocket.

I put everything back in the suitcase and zipped it. I scanned the room some more but nothing else jumped out and screamed CLUE!

Ainsley looked like she was going to pee herself.

"Okay. Let's go," I said. I closed the door carefully behind me and locked it.

"I can't believe you just did that," Ainsley murmured as we hurried away from the door. She wasn't sprinting but she looked like she wanted to.

"I need you to buy me a little more time," I said.

"What for?"

I pulled the data drive from my pocket and showed it to her. "I'm going to have a look at this and I need you to keep Amadeus busy until I do."

"Holy shit. You *stole* something from him?"

"Borrowed. Go out to the porch. If it looks like he's coming back, distract him."

"How? He'll see right through me."

"Use your actuary powers."

"That's not a thing."

"For gorgeous young women, I think it is. It won't be a problem."

She paused. "You're just flattering me to get me to do what you want."

"It's technically not flattery if it's true. You are gorgeous and Roman Amadeus isn't blind. But you're also clever. That's why I know it's well within your powers to distract him."

She appraised me with the discerning glare she used so often. "Okay. Fine. What do you think you are going to find on there?"

"Hoping I can tell you in a few minutes."

She bit her lip, then nodded. "If he kills me, you'd better avenge me."

"Deal."

When she was gone I headed for my room. I had a tool in my bag I was hoping Waldo could use to access the data drive.

But when I wandered back through the library, I found my room door open and Agent Osborne inside. He was rifling through my overnight bag. He had already tossed the bed and the dresser.

He didn't even look up when I entered.

"If you needed to borrow some toothpaste, you could just ask," I said.

Osborne unceremoniously dumped the remaining contents of my bag on the top of the dresser, mussed it around a little, then tossed the bag to the floor.

"We're searching everyone. Don't take it personally."

"Looks like you're doing a bang up job," I said. "Glad the Warsaw Pendulum is too large to justify a cavity search. You'd be terrifying with latex gloves on."

He moved my sweatshirt aside and paused, staring at something. He picked a book up. I didn't recognize it. He flipped it open to a page that had been marked with a slip of paper. He read something then held the book out toward me.

"Care to explain this?"

There was a handwritten note between the pages. Something scribbled in cursive. I took the book from him. The note between the pages read: *Thought more about what we discussed. Warsaw was a hub. Lots could move through. I have an idea about what. Let's talk it over privately at the next opportunity.- Winston.*

I closed the book. It was one of the WWII history tomes from the library shelves. I recognized the spine.

Osborne was still waiting.

"You know what I know," I said.

"What were you two discussing?" he asked.

"Nerdy history stuff."

I couldn't tell if Osborne was frowning or if that was just how his face looked all the time. He checked his phone and punched a bony finger at the screen a few times. Maybe it was his room-tossing checklist.

I looked around at the mess the floor had become. "If you're looking for a spot to search next, I suggest Roman's room. He'll appreciate your attention to detail."

Osborne didn't look up from his phone. "I've already inspected Mr. Amadeus's quarters."

I frowned. Amadeus's room didn't look like a cyclone had touched down in his dresser drawers. Osborne's technique must vary.

Osborne put his phone away, then pushed past me and stalked out the door. Dracula back on the hunt.

"Waldo. Not all is normal with that man," I said.

"The same could be said of you," Waldo replied. "Would you like me to search the illegally-obtained, inadmissible evidence in your pocket now?"

"Please do," I said. I looked at the old history book in my hand again. "It's time someone around here gave me some answers."

CHAPTER 21

"This device is encrypted with protection that I cannot bypass," Waldo said. "Without connection to my full database, I don't have access to the tools I need."

I swore.

So far, all my purloining of evidence from Amadeus wasn't working.

Waldo's full capabilities were hosted in the onboard computer system of my car these days, and since the Boss was still parked in the garage at the Rose 'n Bridge, it was doing me no good.

"Perhaps you can simply ask Mr. Amadeus what's on the drive," Waldo suggested.

"I don't have high hopes of that conversation going well," I muttered.

The fact that Amadeus had a secret drive meant that whatever it was mattered. It was something he wasn't comfortable hosting on his phone or personal data cloud. His cloud wouldn't have been accessible on Attu anyway, but a separate drive also offered a modicum of protection when it came to plausible deniability. Waldo had at least been able to determine that the encryption wasn't biology-based. No retina or facial recognition software. Nothing to tie it to him personally. Most of the criminals I knew avoided bio-sensing security as a rule. Roman was nothing if not hip with the times.

I started tidying up the mess Osborne had made of my room while I tried to think of another tactic.

Waldo piped up again while I was putting away my clothes. "There is one person on this island who has the anti-encryption tools we need. And she brought her computer with her."

I paused my folding. He was right. Zigzag was the best hacker I knew. She could likely crack Roman's encryption like a walnut. But I still wasn't sure how I felt about asking.

"Zigzag's been acting real strange this trip. I don't know what her deal is, but it's like she's been avoiding me."

"She sought you out last night for the purposes of conversation."

"And ran off right away without telling me why."

"She may have been socially embarrassed at discovering another woman in your bed. Perhaps she presumed you and Miss Parker had engaged in a bit of *interior decorating*."

I squeezed my temples. "Go ahead and scratch that one from the euphemisms list, Waldo."

"She thought you were checking her oil with your dipstick."

"Yes. I get the reference. But I don't think that's what was bothering Zigzag. Something else is going on."

"Are you going to break into her accommodations next?"

"Time will tell." I picked up the book Osborne had found on my dresser.

It didn't surprise me that Winston might have a key to my room. He did run the lodge. But why this book? I flipped it back open to the note, reread it, then scanned the pages he had inserted it between. It wasn't about Attu. It was discussing the Nazis. More specifically a horde of artwork and stolen treasures that Adolf Hitler had acquired in Eastern Europe. Supposedly it had never been found. The page Winston had noted specifically mentioned a rumor that the trove of artifacts was last spotted near Warsaw.

Well, shit. Winston might be onto something.

Things did just go missing sometimes. But a horde of valuables like that would make an attractive target for thieves. Especially time travelers. Was Winston suggesting that the lost Nazi treasure trove was somehow linked with the cache from the Warsaw Ghetto resistance? Why not? Amadeus had found himself an in with an approved relocation project. The time travel authorities had already greenlit Rosen's deal. What if he had put his own mission together and tacked on the relocation of stolen goods? What did he care if he had to foot the bill for some time gates and a lodge if he had a payday like that coming? The time travel authorities wouldn't know that the Warsaw Pendulum was now carrying the location not only of the artifacts from the Jewish resistance, but also a trove of stolen valuables from the Nazis. It was a good plan.

But it was a plan that needed tending to. Amadeus would want to be sure he was there to collect when the relocation agent showed up. Once he had recovered the Nazi treasure, he could pass the Warsaw Ghetto cache on to Rosen or not. He'd already have separated out what he came for.

I picked up the data drive I'd taken from Roman's bag. Was there something on here to link Amadeus to Nazi treasure?

Zigzag was my best chance of finding out.

I went looking for her, but after visiting her room, the kitchen, and the drawing room again, I still hadn't located her. I found no sign of Winston either. That was odd. Maybe they were together somewhere.

Roman and Leo were still on the porch smoking their cigars. Ainsley was leaning on the railing giving them her best smiles. I spotted Fallgrave in an armchair in the salon. Thinking? Having a siesta? Whatever it was, he was there. Mary Hurst was in the kitchen still. She looked up as I walked by but went back to her work immediately.

Where the hell was Zigzag?

I finally checked the aviary. I hadn't been in here during daylight hours. There were trees in here. Only ones on the island I imagined, sitting in pots and on long rows of tables. Fruit trees maybe. There were structures approximating trees as well, long rails for perches and there were actually birds. They were all up at the highest points in the room, watching me. I couldn't have said what they were. Some finches maybe? One was a breed I was sure I'd never seen before, with a black-and-white striped head and yellow breast. There was a small pool too, the black plastic kind used for making backyard ponds. It was filled with only a few inches of water and some floating plants, and sat on one of the black tables.

But nothing was moving. The birds just stared from the heights. No birdsong. No chirps of warning. No splashing in the pond. The silence was eerie.

"What's the deal here, birds?" I asked.

There was a rake lying in an aisle beyond the next raised table of plants. The metal prongs were pointed to the ceiling. I approached with the intention of picking it up, but when the rest of the handle came into view between the tables, so did the feet.

I moved around the corner of the table and found the prostrate figure of Winston Carlisle.

He had a kitchen knife lodged in his back.

CHAPTER 22

I just stared for a while. Too long. I finally crouched to check his vitals, but I already knew.

There was a lot of blood. It was pooled around Winston's torso. I put a hand out to the leg nearest me and felt the ankle for a pulse. I didn't find one. Winston's skin was still plenty warm though.

You learn a few things about death in my business, and one is that the human body cools roughly a degree and a half every hour after death. I didn't have a thermometer on me, but I shouldn't need one. I'd seen Winston alive not long ago. But he was also a time traveler. Didn't hurt to be thorough.

"Waldo, I need you to do some work." I pulled my shades out and slipped them on.

"Opening your forensics applications," Waldo said.

I started to run some scans.

"Mr. Travers." I turned to find Fallgrave in the doorway. "May I have a word?"

He likely couldn't see the body from there.

"You need to see this," I said. "Winston Carlisle is dead."

Fallgrave limped forward, leaning heavily on his cane. He

stopped next to me and stared. Some of the color went out of his face.

"Just found him. No pulse. I'd guess he's been dead less than an hour."

Fallgrave's gaze seemed fixated on the knife.

"Natural causes, obviously."

He pulled a handkerchief from his pocket and held it to his nose. "I don't think now is the time for jokes, Mr. Travers."

Primary flaccidity in Winston's body had let some things pass. But Fallgrave had to have seen a hundred dead bodies in his career. Maybe he had a sensitive stomach. He kept the handkerchief to his face.

"I'm going to fetch Osborne," he said, and hurried back the way he came. I stared after him.

I moved around the far side of Winston's body and crouched to get a look at his face. "What did you get yourself into, buddy?"

His eyes were still open. His hand was stretched out to one side. Almost like he'd been reaching for something at the end.

I looked under the table in the direction he'd been looking.

Near a circular floor drain under the table, lay one of his painted Japanese soldier figurines.

Another casualty of Attu.

I picked up Winston's arm just a little to check his mobility. No rigor mortis yet. Another sign he died in linear time. If someone had killed him elsewhen and deposited him here, it probably would have taken longer. Maybe enough time for the body to stiffen. I noted my findings on my phone.

When Osborne arrived, he surveyed me skeptically but didn't bother to ask any questions.

"Clear out. If you want to make yourself useful, gather the others. I want everyone in the drawing room and accounted for. Stay there till I say otherwise."

"You don't want my statement?" I asked.

"Looking to confess?"

"Just doing the job."

"Do it in the drawing room. With the others."

I left.

Mary Hurst was my first stop, but I didn't find her in the kitchen. I checked the pantries and poked my head out the door to the porch. No sign of her. While I was checking the porch I spotted Zigzag. She was downstairs at the time gate with her computer plugged in.

"Hey!" I shouted.

She looked up.

"Need you upstairs."

"I'm busy."

I made my way to the back steps and walked down.

She watched my approach with a wary eye. "I'm running another test on the locking system, seeing if there is a way around it."

I looked up at the clouds. Smelled like rain.

"Winston Carlisle is dead."

Her head snapped around. "What?"

"In the aviary. Knife in his back."

"Holy fuck."

"Yeah."

She stared at the lodge for a bit, processing. She slowly looked back to her computer screen, then hit cancel on something. Her movements sped up as she unlinked it from the time gate.

Zigzag was small but there was something tough about her. I could sense her tension. A hardness came into her eyes as well. "We need to get the hell out of this place."

"What did you know about this job coming in?"

She folded her computer into her satchel. "I knew I'd get paid."

"When I showed up you seemed surprised. How come?"

She finally met my eye. "Look, whatever mess you're in here, I'm not the one at fault. This was just a job."

"Winston's dead. That part of the job?"

She clenched her bag close and glared at me. "You're one to talk."

"What do you mean?"

"This is all going to shit," she muttered.

"There's something you're not telling me and I need to know what it is."

"I don't know what the hell is going on anymore, okay? That make you happy?" She glanced up at the porch.

It was hard to know if Roman and Leo were still outside. We were covered by an overhang here and a fair distance around the corner from the chairs outside the drawing room, but it didn't hurt to be careful.

I lowered my voice. "I need to know if I can trust you."

"Why?"

"Because you're the only one on this island who can help me." I reached into my pocket and pulled out the circular data drive I'd taken from Roman's room.

She shrank away slightly. "What is that?"

"That's what I need to find out. There may be a reason Roman is on Attu that he isn't sharing. And I think Winston being dead could be part of it."

"Roman? You took that from Roman? Hell no. I'm not touching it."

"I think whatever he is here for is worth killing over."

"Roman Amadeus doesn't make enemies. He makes dead people," she whispered. "I'm not going to be next."

"We're on Attu. He's stuck the same as we are. He's not a crime boss here. He's a man who needs to pay for his crimes."

"I'm not part of your plan for justice or whatever. Roman is a bad guy. Fine. I give no shits. Not my problem."

"What about Winston? Was he a bad guy?"

Her mouth hardened into a line.

"What about Mary Hurst? Who else is going to die if we don't stop Roman?"

She looked back to the lodge porch, then swore again. Then she stepped forward and swiped the data drive from my hand. "You never stop, do you?"

"I'm going to round up the others. Osborne wants us all in the drawing room. Let's talk after."

"There ever going to be a time I run into you that I don't regret?"

"First time for everything. Maybe the next one."

She hustled off the way I'd come, the data drive squirreled away in her pocket. I waited thirty seconds, then made my way around the edge of the lower level and across the gravel path toward the front steps. As I climbed I noted the chairs in the far corner of the lodge where Ainsley had been talking to Roman and Leo.

Only Roman was there now. He watched me as I took each step.

I reached the top and returned his gaze.

Roman slowly took the stub of cigar from his mouth and pressed it into the arm of the chair.

We both watched it smolder.

CHAPTER 23

Rain pelted the front windows of the drawing room.

Ainsley was crying softly on the couch.

Everyone knew about Winston.

Presumably, one person in the room knew before I told them, unless Winston had somehow managed to bury that knife in his own back.

Fallgrave and Osborne had done a preliminary investigation and were having a discussion about how they'd get a medical examiner in.

If the tachyon pulse transmitter ever went back together, more agents could be called and they could be instructed to arrive now, prior to even being called. It was a tricky bit of time travel to pull off and avoid paradoxes, but in extreme cases it could be authorized.

This had all the makings of an extreme case, but as the minutes ticked by, no one from the future arrived to take over the situation.

That meant something.

It meant the future wasn't going according to plan. Or maybe Time Crimes had other reasons for staying out of it.

All we knew for now was that we were alone.

Fallgrave and Osborne had done their due diligence. They proposed a timeline, established where everyone was for the last couple of hours and had asked the right questions.

It turned out I was the last one to see Winston alive. Then I was the first one to see him dead.

Those circumstances weren't lost on me. More than once I found Fallgrave's scrutinizing stare lingering in my direction. They had to know soon enough. Time Crimes detectives were typically issued personal time travel devices for a case like this, a Temprovibe or something similar. One of them could use it, go back in time and observe. Unlike the shooting of Logan Tyler, we had an indoor location for Winston's death. Easier jump conditions. We had a body this time too. Whoever stabbed Winston had to have known it would be easier to watch, but they couldn't plan for all eventualities.

But then why weren't they headed back for a look yet? I'd have at least planted some micro-cameras around the aviary by now.

Osborne and Fallgrave were still whispering in the corner, casting the odd glance at the rest of us.

I wandered over to where Zigzag was sitting. She'd taken her spot in the chaise lounge again, a seat that notably kept a wall to her back and everyone else where she could see us. I didn't blame her. She had her laptop open but the glow on her face may as well have been a spotlight on her tension.

I sat on the edge of the lounge near her feet but close enough that we could hear each other at a whisper. "You have time to look at what I gave you?"

"Now? Here?"

"I need to know."

Roman and Leo looked in our direction once, but went back to their own low conversation. Mary Hurst sat at the sideboard fiddling with the silver nutcracker again. The big wooden bowl was still half full of nuts but she must not have been hungry. She just squeezed the nutcracker over and over, occasionally testing it on her knuckles.

Ainsley watched me between sniffles. Her expression was hard to read. Sadness over Winston, sure. But her reddened eyes flitted between Zigzag and me with a look of something else. Jealousy? Maybe she thought I should be on the couch helping her cry.

Zigzag tapped on her keyboard. She was wearing smart lenses that made her eyes glow blue. "Encryption isn't bio. That's a plus."

I knew that already, so I waited.

"I'm going to try a custom program I made. But it'll take a few."

Osborne and Fallgrave finished their whispered conversation and made their way over. Zigzag closed her laptop.

Fallgrave rubbed the top of his cane with his thumb. "Mr. Travers, we'd like a private word. Please join us in the salon."

I rose.

Fallgrave's makeshift office was becoming a familiar location. He took a seat behind the desk and using both hands, crossed his bad leg over his other knee. Osborne stood behind me.

"Do you have anything else you'd like to say about the events of this weekend that you have yet to share?" Fallgrave asked.

"Such as?"

"What Winston Carlisle was so eager to talk to you about?"

Osborne would have told him about the note.

"I think it's possible that Roman Amadeus has hijacked this project for his own ends. He may be using the transport of the Warsaw Pendulum as cover for a requisition of other historical artifacts."

"You have any proof of this?"

"Not yet," I admitted. "Just a theory."

"But Winston Carlisle believed this to be true as well?"

"We were discussing the possibility. I think he may have found something else to verify it, but it's hard to ask him now."

"And you suspect Roman Amadeus in his death."

"Could be. Maybe he figured out Winston was onto him."

"We have a witness verifying Roman's whereabouts during the time of Carlisle's murder."

"Sure. Ainsley was talking to him and Leo on the porch."

"You see how that presents a problem."

I nodded. "It means he hasn't done it yet. And now we have to give him access to his chronometer again if we hope to avoid a paradox."

"We are all in agreement that Roman Amadeus is the most likely suspect in this case. Our investigation thus far has left little doubt. However, the Temporal Crimes Investigations Division has very specific rules about this sort of thing. We cannot arrest someone for a crime they haven't yet committed."

"But if you give Amadeus his chronometer and let him go back in time to kill Winston, you'll likely never see him again."

Fallgrave fidgeted with his cane some more. "Our best chance of making a case against Mr. Amadeus in the deaths of Winston Carlisle and Logan Tyler is to observe but not interfere. There is a high probability that interference could disrupt the timeline and duplicate it. All of us ending up in a parallel reality would solve nothing. If we intentionally or accidentally saved Carlisle and Logan from death, it would only serve to create a paradox in which their original murders become impossible to prosecute and it would potentially leave all of us in a permanent state of duplication. This is a problem I know you in particular would be keen to avoid."

"But if you tell Roman you are onto him, that may scare him off the job. If he fails to go do the killings you suspect him of, that could create a paradox or duplicate the timeline just as easily."

"You see how sticky of a problem this is for us to resolve, especially without the full resources of TCID at our disposal."

Osborne was still looming over my shoulder. I gave him a wary nod. "So what do you need me for?"

Fallgrave placed both hands over the lion head knob of his cane and rocked it back and forth. "Agent Osborne and I have developed a ruse in which we hope to lure Mr. Amadeus into a false sense of confidence. But in order to successfully fool him, we are going to need your help."

I put my hands on my hips. "Shit. You need a fall guy."

"Only temporarily. We shall make it appear that you are the accused in this case. When the time gate unlocks, I shall go back in time for the purposes of observing the crimes. It shall seem to those here, that I have communicated to Agent Osborne my findings, and he shall arrest you. Once Amadeus believes he's in the clear and has been given his chronometer, I propose that he will go back in time to commit the crimes, knowing that you will be the one to pay the price. We shall give him just enough information to believe he can pull off the murder but will, in fact, have given himself away."

"You'll still have to catch him."

"We'll have agents standing by, ready to pursue. Agent Osborne has already searched Mr. Amadeus's belongings and identified any anchors he may attempt to use for escape. He won't get far."

"Why wait till the time gate unlocks? Don't one of you have a Temprovibe you can use? Why not just travel back in time on your own?"

Osborne and Fallgrave shared a glance, but Fallgrave put up a hand. "Agent Osborne and I are experiencing a technical difficulty that we have hoped to keep discreet. The units we brought are not programmed to operate in this particular timestream. As you are likely aware, Temprovibe technology is notoriously glitchy when it comes to use on off-Grid locations. We seem to have encountered such a glitch."

I had heard the rumors. Another reason I stuck to using a chronometer or the Boss for my jumps. But I'd expected Time Crimes to have a better grip on their tech. I sighed. "Okay. So this is the best plan you've got?"

"The plan is excellent," Osborne intoned.

Easy for him to say. He wasn't the one being set up as a murderer.

"Fine," I said. "If it takes Amadeus down, I'm game. Let's make me a killer."

CHAPTER 24

There were still a couple of hours till the time gate unlocked.

After my plotting with Fallgrave and Osborne, I wandered the lodge mulling my options. I wasn't in love with the idea of getting arrested, temporarily or not. But I had to admit we were in a bind.

"You are uneasy again," Waldo said in my ear.

"I don't like this situation," I muttered. "Makes me twitchy."

"Why not offer an alternative solution?"

"Don't have one."

Tyler's and Carlisle's killer held all the control right now. Amadeus was currently untouchable.

I'd left Zigzag in the drawing room, but I was hoping she'd have an answer to my questions soon.

I avoided the aviary in my wanderings. As far as I knew, Winston's body was still in there. Looking through the glass door from the hall, I could just make out the edge of a tarp they'd used to cover him. Least they could do, I guess.

It was still raining. Figured.

I took a walk around the porch anyway. It was cold, but I needed it. Some fresh air to clear my head.

Fallgrave's plan could work. If Zigzag could prove Roman

Amadeus was hiding something else in the Warsaw Pendulum shipment, we had a motive for him to kill Winston Carlisle and Logan Tyler. He had a chronometer, therefore had the means to jump around in time to commit the crime. All he needed now was the opportunity.

"You think something is going to go wrong," Waldo said.

"Maybe. I don't know. Something just feels wrong."

"You found a fault in the inspector's logic?"

"No. But sometimes doing nothing to stop a killer feels a lot like aiding in a murder."

"It bothers your conscience? You know the murders have already happened. You can't change the past."

"I know. Doesn't change the feeling."

Waldo was right. I'd seen Winston's body. He was dead and there was no way to change it, even if I had developed an affinity for the guy. What happened happened. It was the first rule of time travel. I'd heard it echoed since I was a kid. Not that I'd always listened.

But I knew where that had gotten me too. Somewhere out there in time was another me. The other Greyson Travers living the life I could have been living, the product of my failure to play by the rules. I felt the familiar nagging in my gut. The unease at the memory. It wasn't regret. I'd made my choice. I'd do the same again. But I was living with the consequences.

I stared at the rain falling over Attu and tamped down the memory. It wasn't what I needed. This wasn't the time for more paradoxes either. I'd play the game. Roman would go down, I'd retrieve what I came for, then head home.

Home.

I shook my head. I hadn't been at the Rose 'n Bridge anywhere long enough to be calling it that. But I recognized the feeling. The memory of Heavens' face came unbidden. The way her lips had looked when they were so close to mine. It wasn't such a bad place to stay. Not that I'd have to if I finished this job. I'd be loose again. Untethered.

For some reason the thought didn't bring the usual relief. Maybe I'd been untethered so long it had lost its ability to thrill.

I found I was staring at the patch of ground a dozen yards from the porch overhang. I tilted my head. Only then did I recognize what I'd been staring at. Those looked like footprints. In the mud.

They came from the broad sea of grass and headed for the lodge.

"What on earth?" I muttered.

Everyone was indoors. Who would have come in from outside?

I looked over the porch railing to the lower story. Far to the right was the time gate, the truck backed out of the rain under the overhang.

I'd been down there a few hours ago with Zigzag. I was sure there hadn't been footprints in the mud then. There hadn't been mud then. And the rain would have washed them away in any length of time in this downpour.

Those footprints were recent.

I leaned over the porch railing farther. My head and collar were getting soaked. I pulled back and shivered. But I moved to the stairs just the same, back the way I came and down the steps. When I reached the ground level, I ducked out of the rain and studied the earth under the overhang.

There were wet spots on the gravel. Flecks of mud.

I followed.

The trail led around the base of the lodge. It was dark under here. The porch terminated against a wall above me, but there was a path that continued on the ground floor. A wooden door was ajar here. It had a latch but no lock was in evidence. A storage shed of some kind?

I unhooked the latch and opened the door. A few patio chairs were stacked in one corner near the door, but the dim light of the outdoors failed to penetrate farther. I fumbled for my flashlight. I'd left it in my coat upstairs. I settled for my shades. "Waldo, activate low light lenses."

My view brightened, but not by much. As I stepped into the storage space, I was met with almost complete darkness. There were crates down here. Ahead of me was a stack of discarded shipping pallets. Made sense. Wood was a valuable commodity on this island. No use wasting it. And where was there to throw anything away anyhow? I suspected Mary would burn most of the trash we used after we'd left. I'd seen a fire pit out back. Maybe this was fuel for the bonfire.

But there was more down here too. Including mud on the floor. I stooped and picked up a clump the size of a blueberry. It was still wet.

"Hello?" I said to the darkness.

A crash came from the back of the room. I ducked instinctively, then listened. Running feet. A scrabbling sound.

I rushed forward, pushing further into the dark, my hand out. I fumbled for my phone. I needed a better light. I finally got it out of my pocket and shone it in the direction of the crash. My lenses flared. Auto-adjusting to the brightness, but not fast enough. Someone scrambled through a crawl space window in the far corner. It banged shut behind them.

Shit.

I ran around the piles of crates and boxes but was met by a maze of junk. It took me long enough to get to the crawl space window that I was too late to see anything. Whoever had gone through was no longer in view. I shone my light into the crawlspace. It was a low passage. Just an access opening. There were numerous pipes protruding from the floorboards above. Big ones. Looked like it was under the aviary.

I did a quick scan of the corner I was in. There were several blankets on the floor. Some books. Books? And then I spotted the glass dish with brown crumbs adhered to the sides. I crouched and had a closer look. It was the dish of brownies.

I studied the area some more. A lantern. The missing champagne bottle. Someone had been hiding down here. One of the book covers looked familiar. I picked it up. It was "Body of Evidence" by Constantine Fallgrave.

"What the hell?" I muttered.

I studied the book jacket, then shone my light back into the crawlspace hole.

There was someone else on this island, and they were either trying to solve this case, or they were a killer.

CHAPTER 25

The click of a camera sounded from beside me. Mary Hurst snapped a picture of the mess in the storage room.

"Can't be sure what we're dealing with here," Fallgrave said. "Osborne will process the scene and see if we can come up with anything useful."

Osborne was still upstairs at the moment, keeping an eye on the others. Mary Hurst had insisted on seeing the space, however.

"Some nerve they have," she muttered and snapped another photo.

"You know this space was down here?"

"It had a padlock on it when I arrived. I don't have the key."

Wasn't how I found it. I studied the scene some more. "At least they liked your brownies."

I'd already done a walk around, scouting other spaces outside the lodge that might present places to hide. I'd located three more crawl space access covers, two of which were unattached. There were boot prints around each. Some recent. I'd been thoroughly drenched for my efforts but felt I had a better grasp of the situation. Whoever this person was, the footprints showed they'd left by one of the other openings and run off into the rain again. Not even Fallgrave was in a mood to pursue.

"We could be dealing with some form of vagrant," he mused.

"Anyone marooned on this island would have taken up residence in the lodge and come running at the first sign of other people," I argued. "Why hide unless they have something to do with our situation?"

"I suppose time will tell," he said.

His suggestion might have been a test. See if I'd go along with it. It was absurd to think some kind of island hobo would choose Fallgrave's book out of all the options in the library.

I made my way back upstairs and headed to my room to shower. Stripping out of my wet clothes felt good. The hot shower water ran over me and pulled the chill from my bones. I stayed longer than normal in the stream, just enjoying the heat. By the time I toweled off, I felt like a new man.

When I walked out into my room I jolted.

Ainsley Parker was sitting on my bed.

"Holy hell," I muttered, covering myself with the towel. I missed privacy.

"I'm scared," she said, sliding off the bed and walking over to me. She wrapped her arms around my waist and pressed the side of her face to my chest.

I sighed, then gave her shoulder a couple quick pats. "You'll be all right. I promise."

"There has been some weirdo in the basement this *whole* time. Don't you think we should just stay in here till the time gate unlocks? I locked the door. They won't make us come out, will they?" She squeezed me a little tighter. "That killer is out to get us."

"We don't actually know that."

"What?" She pulled away slightly. "How do we not know? They already killed twice. We're lucky we weren't all murdered in our sleep last night."

I tied the towel around my waist. Ainsley watched.

"We have armed cops here now."

"I don't trust them like I trust you." She pressed herself against me again. "They didn't save Winston."

She had a point. Though I hadn't managed to protect him either.

It was obvious she was finding a little comfort in my presence, but it was going to be difficult to put clothes on with her attached to me.

She seemed content just holding onto me so I draped my arms over her and let my mind wander.

We'd have to find our secret resident sooner or later. It was still raining out there. Whoever they were, they'd be wet and cold. Where would they go? There wasn't much around here in walking distance. Mary had mentioned a utility shed where they kept the four-wheeler. I could check there. And there was the floatplane. My eyes drifted to the window.

"If this psycho comes back, you'll protect me, right?"

I looked down to find Ainsley staring up at me, her eyes wide and lips slightly parted. Vulnerable.

"Yeah."

"Can't we just stay in here? At least for a little? Don't go."

I sighed. "Okay."

That seemed to be all the confirmation she needed. She ran her hands up to my neck, rose on her tiptoes and kissed me. Her lips were soft. Benefits of all that cherry lip gloss.

She pressed her whole body against mine and put one of her hands to the back of my head, her fingers in my hair.

"I want you to know I appreciate it," she whispered.

Her other hand trailed down my back. After a moment, I felt it slip under the edge of my towel. Next I knew, the towel was on the floor. Ainsley started pulling me toward the bed, her mouth and hands all over me. She worked fast. She paused to whip off her sweater and was back up against me in a flash. Her bra was hot pink. She started pulling me toward the bed again. She'd made an interesting choice for a handle.

But a sudden image flashed in my head.

"The books," I murmured.

"What?" Ainsley panted, her breath hot in my ear.

I took Ainsley by the waist and pushed her onto the bed. She looked momentarily delighted, but then her expression changed as I started looking for my clothes. "I need pants."

"Wait. What? Why?"

But I'd found my duffel bag and extracted boxer shorts and a pair of jeans. I pulled them on. "There's something I need to check."

I headed for the door, flinging it open and walking barefoot and bare-chested into the library. Osborne had left the pile of books we'd found downstairs on one of the library tables. I grabbed the first one and checked the cover. More WWII history. Not a surprise. We had a ton of those in this collection. But I skimmed through it, comparing it to the one Winston had found. It didn't take me long. I found several pages dog-eared. There was nothing in the marked pages about the Warsaw resistance, but I found several paragraphs describing a train loaded with Nazi gold that reportedly went missing near Walbrzych. According to subsequent research, the existence of the train had been written off as an urban legend. Despite several deathbed confessions of Nazi soldiers who had attested to having seen the treasure, no sign of it had ever been found. The second book was dog-eared at the same story, only a slightly different telling.

Our uninvited basement guest had been doing the same research Winston had.

I wondered what that said about their longevity. Or mine.

"What is it? What are you looking at?" Ainsley asked. She'd snatched up her sweater to follow me but hadn't put it on yet.

"Still trying to figure that out," I said. "But I'm pretty sure the

Warsaw Pendulum is the key to a lot more than just the cache from the Warsaw Ghetto." I reached for the last hardback on the table. It was the copy of Fallgrave's book, "Body of Evidence." I skimmed through it but found no dog-eared pages. I recognized the text well enough, having read the book so often, but nothing was jumping out at me as especially relevant. Finally I turned the book over and studied the back cover copy. It was full of accolades from other writers and had the same author photo of Fallgrave I'd seen on all his books. It was a dramatic black-and-white shot that showed him darkly shadowed by his Cuban hat, the studio lighting only falling on the silver of his mustache and flaring off the polished brass lion head of his famous cane. The definition on the lion head was worn almost smooth from use. It was a stylish photo. He certainly looked mysterious.

What interest did our guest have in the book? Crash course on detective work?

I was missing something. I could feel it in my core. What was it?

"Oh my God," Ainsley said, clutching her sweater to her chest.

I turned and found Agent Osborne entering the room with his gun drawn. Inspector Fallgrave was on his heels. Osborne glared at Ainsley, then pointed the gun at me. "Grayson Travers, put your hands up. You are under arrest for the murder of Winston Carlisle."

CHAPTER 26

I'd been handcuffed to the armchair in the drawing room for over an hour now. They hadn't even let me put on a shirt. I was grateful Mary had stoked the fire again. At least I wouldn't freeze.

Perhaps the most significant change to the room had come in the form of the time gate. With Winston's safety concerns for the lodge no longer a factor, Agent Osborne had enlisted the help of Leo in dismantling the framework of the gate and transporting it upstairs. They had reassembled it in the doorway leading to the salon. The doorframe now bristled with temporal wave emitters.

It would have been a messy business employing the gate in the rain outdoors anyway. No one had voiced any complaints about the location change.

It hadn't taken long for Fallgrave and Osborne to spin their tale for the benefit of the others.

They claimed my fingerprints had been found on the knife in Winston's back, along with those of Mary Hurst who I'd presumably taken it from. She confirmed she had seen me in the kitchen with Ainsley before Winston's death. It was possible I could have taken the knife.

Ainsley reluctantly admitted that I had sent her away after

that, out to talk to Roman and Leo on the porch. She hadn't been with me during the presumed time of Winston's death and the three of them being together all made for airtight alibis.

I'd been found with Winston's body. That spoke volumes.

As to my motive?

Osborne provided that. He claimed Winston himself had expressed concerns about me during his interview. He felt in danger and that I was there to hijack the project, steal the pendulum for myself, and leave everyone else out of it. That was an obvious fabrication, but it wasn't like anyone else would know. It added threads to the narrative.

The part that was hard to listen to was when they pressed Ainsley regarding the shooting the night we arrived. Had the man in the fog who did the shooting been my height and size? She reluctantly agreed that he had been. At least she said it with a tear in her eye.

Had anyone actually been with me in the fog at the time of the shooting? Everyone could truthfully say they hadn't.

I had to admit the picture of my guilt they were painting was starting to look pretty good.

The grandfather clock in the foyer had already struck seven a while ago. In a few minutes the time-locked safe in the library would unlock and the chronometers would be available.

Roman was looking smug.

Mary Hurst didn't seem to have taken the news as a particular surprise. I got the impression it took a lot to ruffle her.

"And if anyone else has information that can confirm Mr. Travers' guilt, I suggest you share it now." Fallgrave made a big show of staring down each person in the room.

Ainsley cracked under his gaze. "He stole something. From Mr. Amadeus's room. Some kind of data drive."

I groaned. My actual misdeeds weren't supposed to be part of this play.

It got a response from Roman. He stood. "What drive?" He glared at me.

"Is there something on the drive that pertains to this case?" Fallgrave asked.

"Nothing," Amadeus snapped. He approached my chair. "Where is it?"

But I didn't get a chance to reply.

"I have it." Zigzag held up a hand from her seat on the chaise lounge. She was holding the drive.

Fallgrave's brow furrowed. "And just what were *you* doing with it?"

"Travers wanted me to hack into it, see what was on it." Zigzag looked directly at me as she spoke, her gaze unwavering. I stared back.

"And did you?" Fallgrave asked.

"Of course not. That would be illegal."

"Finally. Someone with some sense," Roman said. He flicked his finger and Leo lumbered over to Zigzag. She dropped the drive into his meaty hand.

"I'd like to know what is of such importance on this drive of yours," Fallgrave said.

"And when you have a warrant for such, I suppose you might," Roman replied. "But since we have been unable to communicate with the outside world, I can assume you have no such permission." Leo handed him the drive and he pocketed it.

Fallgrave stroked his mustache. Then he straightened. "It matters little. We are long overdue for a resolution to this entire case. In a few minutes the time gate will unlock and we will have it. I will pass through to a time prior to the shooting that brought us here. I shall observe the events and report back as to the nature of the event. I believe it will leave little doubt as to the guilt of Mr. Travers. But should it become necessary, I will make a second jump and surreptitiously record him in the act of murdering Mr. Winston Carlisle. While I am at it, I can ascertain the identity of the person scurrying around in the basement."

"Then we can all depart this godforsaken island," Amadeus replied.

"However," Fallgrave added, "you will all remain here under the supervision of Agent Osborne until my return. At no point will anyone attempt to leave this island without my authorization."

Roman rolled his eyes but didn't comment.

My wrists were chafing in the cuffs. I was fine with play acting, but I was getting tired of sitting in this chair. I was half ready to *confess* my guilt if they'd just let me walk around a little.

"Let's get this show on the road," Leo said. He walked behind Osborne and snatched a bottle of Vodka from behind the bar. He began pouring himself a drink. Osborne eyed him skeptically for a moment, then brought his attention back to the gate. "It's set up. The coordinates are ready."

"Aren't you forgetting something?" Roman said. He tapped his wrist.

"Not a thing," Fallgrave replied, checking his watch. "Mary, I'd like you to go to the library and retrieve the chronometers belonging to Mr. Amadeus and Mr. Travers. The safe should unlock momentarily. Bring them to me."

Mary rose from her chair. She gave me a quick glance, but if she was feeling any sympathy for my situation, it didn't show. She walked out.

Made sense to send a linear. She was the only one Fallgrave could trust not to use one of the chronometers herself.

I'd only met Amadeus once before and had never seen him anything but calm. But now there was something else brewing just beneath the surface. Something murderous? His exterior calm only made him seem more dangerous.

Fallgrave didn't seem to notice.

"I have instructed Agent Osborne to detain everyone in this room until I'm back. However much time I need in the past, I will return in the next five minutes via the chronometer."

"If anyone sees you back there, we are all in deep shit," I said. "You're confident you can stay undetected?"

"I've been doing this job decades longer than you've been alive. I hardly think I need advice from a man such as yourself."

It was the response I expected, but I still had my concerns. He was an old man with a cane, working terrain that would require speed and stealth. But at least he had experience.

Mary Hurst returned and brought the two chronometers to Fallgrave. He examined each and selected mine to use. He tossed the other to Osborne, who caught it one-handed.

At that moment something blinked on the time gate control panel.

"Ah. Eight o'clock," Fallgrave said. "We're right on schedule."

He activated the time gate jump scheduler and used his notes to input coordinates. The time gate emitters came to life and shot streams of multicolored light at one another across the doorway. In a matter of seconds the entire space was pulsing and shifting with color. I had to squint to keep watching.

"This shall all be over momentarily," Fallgrave said. "Await my return." He stepped through the gate and vanished.

The emitters powered down after he passed through. I was left blinking at the afterglow, the silhouette of Fallgrave still playing across the inside of my eyelids.

Then came the smash.

I turned in time to see Obsorne's eyes roll back in his head. He went down like a felled tree and left Leo standing behind him with the cracked vodka bottle. He looked at it, then tossed it behind the bar. "How do you like that, copper?" he muttered.

Ainsley shrieked.

Amadeus smiled.

Leo leaned over Osborne's prone body and came back up with a gun in one hand and Roman's chronometer in the other. He tossed the chronometer to his boss, who caught it deftly, then calmly snapped it onto his wrist. Amadeus adjusted his shirt sleeves and jacket. "It's about time."

CHAPTER 27

I had to give it to him. For being a big guy, Leo worked fast when he wanted to.

By the time the rest of us had gotten over the shock of him knocking out Osborne, he had the agent trussed up on the floor like a Thanksgiving turkey.

Osborne had several guns on him. One of which was now in Roman's hand.

"I'd like to advise everyone to remain calm," Roman said. "This won't take long if everyone cooperates." He waved his gun vaguely in the direction of the time gate. "We have a few minutes of messy business, but I have a feeling none of you are going to give me trouble about it." He addressed this to Mary and Ainsley. Ainsley had assumed her terrified position half-buried in the couch cushions again. Mary slowly took a seat on the other end of the same couch.

"It's a pity it had to come to this, of course," Roman continued. "But someone has been interfering with progress on this job, and I feel it's becoming a trend." He looked directly at me when he said it. "You couldn't leave it alone, could you, Greyson?"

"Oh. Were you talking to me?" I said. "I tuned out there for a minute."

"Always the bravado." Roman pointed the gun at me. "Leo, go retrieve Greyson's gun from Osborne's room. We're going to need it as well."

Leo nodded and left.

I must have had a questioning look on my face because Roman continued. "We need a legitimate reason for me shooting you. If you pull a gun on me, it makes things easier to explain."

"Even with three witnesses?"

Roman glanced at the couch. "Women are very practical creatures, Greyson. Haven't you learned that? They're much smarter than men like you."

He turned to Ainsley and Mary. "Do either of you two ladies plan to interfere?"

Ainsley's eyes were wide, but neither woman said a word.

He turned back to me and shrugged. "See?"

He hadn't said anything about Zigzag. She was still on the chaise lounge, watching, but likewise immobile. But the fact that he didn't even address her told me something. He knew where she stood already. They'd been on the same side of this from the beginning.

Leo returned and dumped a bag on the coffee table. He rummaged around in it for only a moment, then came up with a couple more guns, one of which was mine. He handed it to Roman.

"So what's the plan?" I asked. "We shoot it out, then you go back and kill the others, or did you do that already somehow?"

Roman shook his head. "I figured you for smarter, Greyson. For all your meddling, you only learn enough to get yourself in trouble."

I shrugged. "That's probably a fair assessment. Still doesn't explain how you expect to play this. Way I see it, you still have a lot of work ahead of you."

"You don't think I knew what you were up to?" Roman said. He gestured to my handcuffs. "This whole bluff of yours? Trying to pin the murders on me? It's amateur at best. I almost regret having to kill you in such a state of ignorance."

"So, you're trying to convince me I was wrong to jump to the conclusion you were a murderer while you're in the process of explaining how you're going to murder me?"

"It's a complicated situation, Greyson. But I do need you to fill in some details about what you've been up to." He tucked my gun into his waistband and toyed with the other he was holding.

"Always happy to chat," I said.

Roman smiled benevolently. "Who killed Winston Carlisle?"

I blinked. "Come again?"

"Win-ston," he enunciated. "I want you to tell me why he was killed."

I was genuinely confused. Why would he think I knew that? I assumed he'd killed him. Or was going to.

Roman sighed, obviously taking my confusion as obstinance.

"Leo, please make Greyson more cooperative."

"Happy to," Leo said. He stepped over, squared himself up, then punched me in the gut.

Oof.

I'd clenched in time but I think he moved my entire chair two inches. I groaned and stayed doubled over till Leo grabbed my hair and pulled my head back.

"We don't have a lot of time, Greyson," Roman said, checking his watch.

"I'd love to help you," I groaned. "But you suck as a person."

Leo clocked me in the side of the face. My chair went over and I hit the floor.

Jesus that hurt.

Stars flitted across my field of vision. Leo sure knew how to punch.

"I don't want you to *kill* him," Roman grumbled.

"Sorry, Boss," Leo said. "Stepped into that one a little too much."

I was still blinking on the floor. But I wasn't the only thing down here. I found myself staring across the carpet at the lion head topper of Fallgrave's cane. The stars in my vision made it look extra magical. It was on the floor near the bookshelf where it must have fallen over. That couldn't be good. How did Fallgrave expect to get around the past without it?

I was wrenched back to a vertical position by Leo, who hoisted my chair back onto its feet.

My head was still swimming. My eyes drifted back to the cane. It was less shiny now. Fewer stars. Actually it was less shiny than I remembered altogether. There was a dark spot on the lion's nose where the gold paint had worn off.

"Let's out with it now, shall we?" Roman said. "I know you were the last one to talk to Carlisle. What did he say? Was it about the shipment?" He chambered a round in his gun and pointed it at my face. "I really don't have all day, Greyson."

I stared down the barrel of his pistol and wondered what kind of afterlife I was in for. Maybe it wouldn't be so bad.

Leo wound up for another punch.

"Stop. That's enough."

We all turned to look at Zigzag. She was standing, her laptop tucked under one arm.

Roman appraised her skeptically.

"You need to let him go now," Zigzag said. "It's time."

Leo laughed.

Roman didn't. He glared at her. "What are you talking about?"

"Last night. In the fog. The shooter. It was him."

Roman and Leo both looked at me. Roman scoffed. "Sure it was him. We all heard that story already." He gestured to Ainsley. "This one said as much. But we're past that laughable ruse now."

Zigzag shook her head. "Everyone knows this girl couldn't see shit from where she was. But I could. I *saw* the shooter. And it was Greyson." She pointed at me. "And he had a black eye."

CHAPTER 28

I'd spent a fair amount of my life confused about things—the complexities of women's emotions for one. I'd never known which armrest in an airplane middle seat belonged to me, and pretty much everything about the sport of cricket seemed ludicrous. There was plenty about normal life I was incompetent to explain. But I was positively baffled by this.

Zigzag and Roman were talking privately at one side of the room while I squinted and tried to make out if Leo had fractured my eye socket. I could still see out of my left eye, but it was definitely starting to swell.

When I looked to the couch, I found Mary Hurst staring at me, her expression as unreadable as ever. Ainsley glanced at me briefly, but looked away, her focus on the time gate, desperation in her eyes. She cast occasional glances around the room too. I got it. She was waiting for Fallgrave to show back up and save the day. Fallgrave had a gun. He'd be a better protector than me at the moment.

But Leo was on guard too, gun at the ready.

The grandfather clock said 8:06 but there was still no sign of the inspector. Maybe he knew something we didn't. I looked back to the cane he'd left on the floor. Had he run into trouble in the past? Roman checked the time and walked back over to glower at me. He addressed Leo. "Okay. Uncuff him."

Leo moved across the room and rifled through the pockets of the still unconscious Agent Osborne till he came up with the keys to my cuffs. He walked back slowly. "You sure about this?"

Roman studied me. He looked genuinely confused. "Why the hell are *you* going to kill Logan Tyler?"

He asked me like I knew.

I had no idea. It was absurd. The entire reason I'd come here was to meet Tyler and bring the Warsaw Pendulum to Rachel Rosen. What reason could I possibly have to shoot the courier?

But playing dumb hadn't worked well so far. Maybe I should make some shit up.

"It's part of the job," I said.

"You've turned assassin now?" He said it as though it disappointed him.

"Figured it pays better than PI work," I said. "Rosen made a good offer. Thought I'd see how your side lives."

Roman leveled his pistol at my face. "I think you are a liar, Greyson Travers."

A bad one apparently. It looked like my number was up.

But then he raised the weapon and rested it against his shoulder. "Yet it seems you are a liar who gets to live a little longer."

Leo moved in and uncuffed me.

I took a breath and rubbed my wrists.

"Was he dressed like this in the fog?" Roman asked Zigzag.

"No. He had that coat from the closet. The one she gave him." Zigzag gestured to Mary Hurst. "Boots too."

"Fetch him whatever you saw him in," Roman said. "Quickly."

Zigzag left the room. She came back a minute-and-a-half later with my clothes and dumped them in my lap. She met my eye as she did, but said nothing.

Roman kept a gun aimed at me as I dressed. "Whatever it is you're up to, you remember this: someone brings me back that pendulum or things get bloody." He nodded to Leo. Leo moved in on the couch.

"Wait, what?" Ainsley squirmed and tried to get away. But Leo reached for her, pinning her flailing arms and dragging her onto the carpet. She shrieked.

"You seem to like this one," Roman said watching Ainsley writhe in Leo's grip. "Who wouldn't? But if you fail to come back with what I want, she'll be the first to die."

Ainsley looked up at me with wide, terrified eyes. Then she glared at Roman. "You bastard!"

Leo clamped a hand over her mouth and the rest of her invectives got muffled. She was tied up as tightly as Osborne. But this time Leo added a gag.

Mary Hurst watched the whole thing like she was a statue, hands folded in her lap.

"Am I going to have any trouble with you?" Roman asked.

She shook her head.

"Good." Roman gestured to the gate. "Okay. Let's get him set up."

Zigzag went to the gate controls and started programming. She turned to me. "The only way this works is if I send you ahead of the inspector. Same location and time. Time gate won't even have time to shut off on that end before he arrives. But you only have seconds at most to get clear before he shows up."

I recalled what she'd said the night before about the confusing timestream signatures. How it looked like it could have been multiple jumps coming in at once. This was why.

"How long will I have till the courier arrives?"

"About forty-five minutes. But I'm guessing you'll be busy."

I ran over the events of the previous night in my head. Someone had gone through the trouble of moving the entire time gate in that time. The truck too. Why would I do that except for the fact that I already had? And was I going to just go ahead and shoot Logan Tyler while I was at it? If I didn't, I'd be looking at a paradox. I could alter time and create a parallel timestream otherwise. It was the last thing on earth I wanted, but did that mean I was ready to go shoot an innocent courier? And where would Fallgrave be during all this? Presumably keeping a low profile, and standing by to arrest me when I was done with it all.

Nothing about this made sense.

Zigzag pressed the power control on the gate and the emitters burst to life. The room was once again bathed in multi-colored light. Leo had dragged Ainsley over near Osborne, presumably to be able to watch them both easily. Ainsley's eyes were brimming with tears and she made more muffled pleas into her gag.

Roman handed me my gun.

Leo had his ginormous pistol drawn and pointed at my head. Roman didn't bother. It wasn't the guns compelling me and he knew it.

I turned to Zigzag. "You're sure this is how it went down?"

"I know what I saw."

Apparently she saw me have a complete personality change and turn into a cold-blooded murderer. I holstered my gun and clipped it to my waistband. It was good to be armed, but I'd have felt better with a chronometer on my wrist too.

I watched the colors swirl around the doorway. Normally I wouldn't mind leaving a place where gangsters and their thugs enjoyed punching me for sport, but somehow I didn't think where I was headed was any less dangerous. There was only one way to find out.

CHAPTER 29

At least this time I didn't land on my ass.

When I stepped through the time gate into what stood for my yesterday, I had very little idea of what to expect.

Looked a lot like the first time I'd come through, only foggier, and with no Mary Hurst to mock me. It only took me half a second to know where I had to hide. There were no other options. I sprinted around the back side of the time gate, dropped to my belly and rolled under the old pickup truck.

I was just in time too. As Zigzag predicted, it was only seconds until Constantine Fallgrave stepped through the time gate.

The emitters shut off behind him and the world dimmed.

I blinked in the fading twilight, my eyes not accustomed to it yet.

Fallgrave's pant legs and shoes were visible, and just the edge of his long coat. I couldn't see much else. He turned around and faced the way he'd come, toward the back end of the pickup. Toward me. I assumed he'd want to get himself out of sight, maybe to a nearby hillside where he could watch the action, or maybe even make a bee line for where he knew the shooting would take place later.

But he didn't do either of those things. He started collapsing the time gate and stowing it in the back of the truck.

What the hell?

Constantine Fallgrave was one of the most decorated detectives in Time Crimes. What was he doing messing around with past events?

As he finished the loading of the time gate in the back of the truck, the realization of what was happening finally began to register. He walked with steady steps to the front of the truck and climbed in. I scrambled out from under the rear of the vehicle just as the engine fired. It was an old column shifter and lurched as he put it into gear. I barely had time to get my hands onto the tailgate and a foot on the rear bumper before the truck was moving. I ducked low, finding purchase with my other foot and hoping to keep my head from view in the rear view mirror. With the time gate frame cluttering up the back of the truck, I assumed he would have a hard time seeing me, but it didn't hurt to be careful.

The old truck bumped and groaned over the rough terrain. It took all of my focus to hold on.

Fallgrave slowed a few times and made turns, orienting himself. He turned a circle and headed in a different direction, changed his mind and turned again. Didn't he know where he was going?

To be fair, it all looked the same in the deepening fog. Not like he had a GPS out here. Eventually he made a decision and drove in one direction for a long stretch. We went up and down a few low hills, but then steadily climbed to the top of a hill I recognized. This was our stop.

By the time the engine shut off, I was back on the ground and away, running in a crouch, not with any particular destination, just away. Far enough that I could throw myself down in the tall grass and have a look back at what was going on.

Fallgrave climbed out of the truck, quicker than I'd seen the old man move before, and he set to work unloading the time gate. He was working efficiently but not rushing. He didn't behave as a man who felt in a hurry or that he was being watched. When he finished the resetting of the time gate, he set it to standby mode and surveyed his work. Seemingly satisfied, he turned and walked off into the grass in the direction of the lodge. The direction he knew the shooting would eventually take place.

Maybe it was the cold and damp. Maybe the fog was affecting my brain. Whatever it was, I felt like it was taking longer than it should for me to process through all this.

Fallgrave was setting this all up the way he'd seen it done on our walk. He'd taken enough photos. He had a gun and was headed for the place we'd seen the blood. It was hard for me to fathom the reasoning behind it, but it left me only one conclusion.

Constantine Fallgrave was going to shoot Logan Tyler.

I pulled my gun and followed him.

What was I going to do? I had no idea. The past was the past, you can't change it.

But this *felt* wrong.

The words Heavens had said came back to me. *If you get in a situation where something doesn't feel right, trust your gut and get out of there.*

I couldn't run. Not now. But I was sure as hell going to do something.

I strode through the tall grass and cut at an angle to intersect the path Fallgrave had taken. I knew where he'd be. So did Waldo. I slipped on my shades and whispered to him. "Activate Breadcrumbs."

Waldo layered my previous trips over my field of vision. There were multiple now. As I scanned the fog, I caught the faint sound of voices in the distance.

The group of us had left the lodge, headed to the original site of the time gate. They'd start searching soon, then head this way when the time gate activated. Waldo showed me the path my earlier self would take. I didn't see myself here the first time. I couldn't now.

This was going to be close quarters.

Part of me knew I ought to leave now. I wasn't here to stop a murder. If Fallgrave or anyone else had killed Logan Tyler here, it wasn't my job to stop them.

I could be a witness though. It didn't mean he had to get away with it.

I walked slowly. Watching. I knew roughly where he'd be. The thick fog muffled sound but occasional snippets of voices drifted up the mountain. I thought I heard myself at one point, directing others to spread out, search for the missing time gate.

I was so focused on the sound, I didn't hear Fallgrave until he'd already approached. I turned to find him watching from about fifteen yards away.

He had his gun leveled at me. "Greyson Travers. Aren't you persistent."

We faced each other across the tall grass, enshrouded by the mist and fog. Fallgrave was wearing low-light lenses too. Mine showed the world with an artificial purple light. His gave his face a yellow glow.

"Do you enjoy torturing yourself, Greyson? You must. It's difficult to be an agent of change in such an unchangeable world."

"You knew this was going to happen," I said. "You planned it."

"How could I not? Don't you admire the logic of it? It's beautiful."

"You're going to kill Logan Tyler and take the pendulum. Then what? Pin it on Amadeus? On me?"

"Pieces of it coming together for you, Greyson? Maybe you do have some promise as a detective yet."

"This could all go bad."

"No. It won't. And certainly not because of you. Don't you know why I selected you for this? You are the one man I knew wouldn't interfere. You're standing there holding a gun, but it does you no good, does it? The future is written."

"It's still changeable."

"By a duplicate? You know more than anyone the price you pay for creating a paradox. I know what you've sacrificed. Family. Friends. It must be horrible to watch another man live the life you should have. And to think of having to do it again? No. You aren't going to change anything here. That's why, when all this is over, I'll request that Rosen sends you personally."

"You haven't done it yet?"

"Not yet. But I will, obviously. Or you wouldn't be here. Like I said. The future is written."

A buzzing hum rose from the time gate. The fog glowed blue, and pink, and red, colors shifting as the emitters pulsed. The night glowed.

"Our guest arrives," Fallgrave said. He put his gun back in its holster but kept his hand on it.

The wait didn't take long. Footsteps in grass. A figure emerged from the fog. She was still wearing clothing from the 1940s, a wool skirt that fell just past her knees and a V-necked jacket buttoned once at the waist. Her hat sat across her head at a rakish angle. The clothing was precise, efficient for the job. She carried a long tube in one gloved hand and held a compass with the other. She saw us and stopped.

"Are one of you who I'm supposed to meet?" she asked. "No one was near the gate." She noted our guns but didn't look alarmed. She'd just come from Nazi occupied Poland. She'd seen worse.

"Ms. Tyler, my name is Inspector Fallgrave from the Temporal Crimes Investigation Division. You've come to the right place."

I sighed. Then I took a few steps and stood between Fallgrave and Tyler.

Fallgrave shook his head. "Don't tell me you're thinking of meddling."

I put a hand on my hip. "You know, I looked up to Constantine Fallgrave for a lot of years. Makes this harder."

He cocked a wry smile. "We must all one day confront the truth of our heroes."

"Can't tell you how many times I looked at that photo on the back of the books and wondered what it might be like to be such a famous detective."

"You've mentioned you were a reader." He kept his eyes on the courier.

"Never could get used to a mustache like that. But it's really the cane that sells it, don't you think?"

"We've wandered a bit off-topic, Mr. Travers. As you know, Ms. Tyler and I have some important business to attend to. It's time for you to step aside." His fingers twitched slightly on the gun at his hip.

"But you didn't bring the cane along for this jump," I continued.

He finally looked straight at me, irritation on his face.

"I saw it lying on the floor when I was getting my face pummeled by Leo after you left. Noticed the chipped gold paint on that lion head too. Funny that it always looked like solid brass in the pictures."

Fallgrave smirked. "You are more observant than I gave you credit for."

"All that talk of logic and reason. You about had me fooled. It was such a Fallgrave thing to say."

He looked angry now. His eyes darted from me to Logan Tyler and back. The clock was ticking.

"All very clever, Greyson. But it doesn't change who *you* are, does it? Or what's *meant* to happen."

I glanced behind me. Logan Tyler looked uneasy now. Questioning. "Thing is, Fallgrave always insisted that good detective work meant solely relying on reason and logic. That's where I disagreed with him. I think every once in a while, you have to trust your gut."

The mustache twitched, then he went for his gun.

I was faster.

I fired.

The bullet caught him in the side before he had time to get his shot off. He staggered back but stayed on his feet. He had a snarl on his lips. He lifted his gun again. "Don't forget . . . there were *two* sh—."

I squeezed the trigger again. My second shot hit him at the center of his chest. He fell backward in the grass.

"Don't worry. I didn't forget."

A woman screamed. But it was distant. Ainsley. Somewhere in the fog.

I couldn't see her from here.

Logan Tyler still clutched the long tube. She held it close to her body but didn't run.

When I walked over to Fallgrave's fallen body, I noticed someone else in the fog beyond him. I raised my gun again instinctively. Zigzag stared at me wide-eyed from a dozen yards distant, but she backed away, retreating quickly into the high grass before disappearing downhill into the fog again.

I picked up Fallgrave's gun from where it had landed and stuck it in my waistband, then I seized both of his wrists and hauled him the few dozen yards to the level patch of gravel I'd seen last night.

"Who are you?" Logan asked, following at a wary distance. "What's going on here?"

"I'm from Rosen. I'm the one you're supposed to meet, but we're in a tight spot. I need you to stick with me and do exactly as I say."

I pushed back the sleeve on the dead man's jacket and removed my chronometer from his wrist.

"This man was a Time Crimes agent?"

"He was impersonating an agent." I bent over the fallen man and took a hold of one end of the bushy mustache. "At least I hope I was right about that."

As I pulled, the false mustache came off in my hand. Logan Tyler looked on in surprise, then she cocked her head. "Wait. Take off his glasses."

I removed the fake Fallgrave's low-light lenses.

"Those eyebrows are false too," she said. "I've seen this man before. His name is Weintraub. He's the one who hired me."

Voices were approaching. Sounded like my earlier self and Ainsley had run into Zigzag.

I tucked the false mustache in my pocket, then gestured for Logan Tyler to come closer. "We've got to go." She approached cautiously. "I need you to grab hold of this guy. Anywhere will do." I set the coordinates and a countdown timer on my chronometer then reached for her hand. She took it. I grabbed a large stone with my chronometer hand and watched the timer tick down.

"Are you making me an accessory to murder?" Logan asked.

"I promise it will all make sense eventually," I said. "Just give me a little time."

My chronometer activated and we vanished.

. . .

I'd jumped us forward an hour. Long enough to get past the flurry of activity that had occurred in the area we were standing.

When we arrived it was still dark. Still foggy.

I would have liked to just jump the entire way back to tomorrow, but it was going to be pouring rain out here during the time I left, and that wasn't how things went down.

Logan Tyler let go of the dead man's clothes and stood. The gravitite particles in our bodies, clothing, and possessions had let us all make the jump, but we'd left the world of an hour ago behind. She appraised me carefully.

"Are we out of danger?"

I rose to my full height as well, and looked in the direction of the lodge. I couldn't see it from here but Waldo had a location flag in my lenses. The Breadcrumbs app was still running.

"We should be safe for now, but we have a bit of walking to do."

"I think you owe me an explanation first," Logan said.

"Things are a little complicated at the moment. I'll do my best to explain, but we need to get you out of sight."

"Are you going to tell me why you shot this man?"

"He was going to kill you."

"Good reason."

"You said you met this guy, Weintraub, before?"

"Not in person. Only over a screen. But I recognize him without the mustache. I was doing what he hired me to do. Why would he want to kill me?"

"If it makes you feel any better, not everyone on the job is trying to kill you. Winston Carlisle had a nice dinner planned. Called you the guest of honor."

"He sounds like a smart man. When do I get to meet him?"

"You don't. Someone is going to stick a knife in his back tomorrow."

"Good hell. What kind of island is this?"

I looked down at Weintraub and contemplated the situation.

"While you were in the past, did anyone approach you about the pendulum?"

Logan shook her head. "It was an easy job. No trouble. Till now."

"Mind if I see it?"

She uncapped the tube. "You have some ID?"

I retrieved the code card Rosen had sent me from my wallet. I handed it to her. She used some kind of scanner on it. It beeped.

"Winner winner." She reached into the tube and retrieved the Warsaw pendulum.

It was bigger than I expected. Roughly a meter long. The bob at the end was ornate, inscribed with a Star of David.

"How is the information coded?

"When you install it in a properly sized clock for thirty minutes, the end will unlock. Coordinates for the location are inside the bob."

I studied the end of the pendulum. "Fascinating craftsmanship. And it explains why they have a grandfather clock in the lodge. Weintraub must have been planning to unlock it here."

Logan looked down at the body. "We going to spend all night with this stiff?"

"The body can stay here for a bit. But I'll need to figure out how to move it by the time my earlier self shows up in the morning."

"You'll be here?"

"Yeah. With him, actually. Might be a bit of a spoiler for his future if he finds his own dead body lying here."

"The relocation agent is supposed to have an exit programmed for me to get home. Don't suppose he bothered with that."

"Considering he planned to kill you? No. I don't imagine so.

The time gate is locked for the next twenty or so hours. We'll need to hide you till then."

She looked around. "In a cozy bed and breakfast nearby?"

I wagged my hand. "How do you feel about old airplanes?"

Logan looked skeptical.

"I also might be able to score you a dish of brownies."

"That's a little more promising."

We left the body of Weintraub where it lay and walked. I used my Breadcrumbs app again and retraced my steps so there wouldn't be extra tracks though the grass in the morning.

While we walked, I explained what was going to happen over the course of the next day. The plan wasn't an especially elegant one. She'd head out to the floatplane and lie low till the lodge was quiet. Eventually she'd be able to make it back to the lodge to hide underneath in the storage area.

It was going to be a night of roughing it, but she didn't complain. Seemed like she was made of tough stuff. I imagined in her business it paid to be adaptable. It would make sense to have her jump back to the future with me, but for some reason that wasn't what happened. Her spending the night in the plane and hiding in the storage area just because she'd already done it smacked of circular logic, but that's all we had to go on.

"What about the pendulum?" Logan asked.

"I'd like you to hang onto it for me if you don't mind. I've got to get the rest of this mess sorted. But when the time comes, I'll need your help."

She listened to my plan and asked only smart questions. We were walking a fine line in regards to how much of her future she should know. I gave her the broad strokes but tried to leave room so that she wouldn't have every moment accounted for. Sometimes the freedom of not knowing what the future holds is what gives you the confidence to live it.

I gave Logan the extra gun I'd pulled from Weintraub too. If anyone else was trying to kill her, she might need it. We weren't done dealing with dangerous people.

We made it close enough to the lodge on our way that I was able to sneak over to the old truck and steal the tire iron from the jack kit.

Then we parted ways. Logan headed Northwest in the direction of the floatplane.

I waited in the fog.

There was still a little time till Fallgrave and Osborne would first arrive via the time gate. I did a careful tour around the bottom of the lodge and checked the storage area door. It was locked.

Couldn't have that. I fished my lock pick set from my pocket and unsnapped the padlock. Now when Logan made her way back she'd have a way in. She already knew where the brownies would be.

I now felt confident that I'd set the right wheels in motion, but this game wasn't over.

Unless I was mistaken, Weintraub hadn't acted alone.

There was still a killer on this island, and I knew right where to find them.

CHAPTER 30

Fun thing about time travel is that you can get right to the point of things. I didn't need a lot of preparation to accomplish what I needed to do. I just needed to think it out.

I stood on the ground floor of the lodge beneath the porch and mulled my options. My earlier self wandered onto the porch above me for a bit. He was busy thinking too.

I waited till he was gone before climbing the porch steps to sneak a peek inside the lodge. The hallway looked clear. I was on the lookout for a good anchor location to jump myself back to the future.

My initial thought was that I'd break into the aviary. It wouldn't hurt to have a look at who killed Winston on the way. But the more I mulled it over, the less convinced I was that I needed to.

Pulling my notepad from my pocket, I consulted my list of suspects by the glow of the doorway.

I ran through the events of the next day in my head. Turned out I knew exactly where everyone on the list was when Winston was killed.

And that gave me an answer I'd been missing.

I checked the time. Right about now my earlier self was

discovering Ainsley Parker in his shower. I wouldn't need to worry about him for a bit. But as I put a hand on the doorknob, I heard voices and had to get myself out of view. There weren't any places to hide on the porch, so I scurried back down the steps, then hid beneath them. The door opened on the porch above and two people came outside.

"You're sure there is no other way to unlock the gate once they arrive?" Winston asked.

"Not the way it's set up." The second speaker was Zigzag. "You're the one who insisted on the lockdown window."

"When we were hosting a celebration of the project's success, it sounded like a grand idea. I didn't expect a shooting."

The pair came down the steps as I shrank back into the shadows.

Zigzag paused at the bottom of the steps and turned to Winston. "Whatever you were told about this job, I think it's changed now."

"I saw your face when Travers arrived. You weren't pleased to see him. Can't we trust him?"

"If you asked me that before today, I would have said yes. Now I'm not so sure." She hesitated, like she was about to say more, but then shoved her hands in her pockets. "I don't think it matters anymore."

They moved off around the corner toward the time gate and I was no longer able to hear their conversation.

I crept back up the steps and slipped inside the lodge.

I felt a twinge of guilt as I passed the aviary. Winston seemed a good man and it was hard knowing I couldn't keep him from dying tomorrow. But I could bring his killer to justice.

A light was on in Roman's room. As was Leo's. I walked past both doors quietly and made my way to the central foyer near the stairs. The tachyon pulse transmitter was there and it looked like it still had all of its parts. Our saboteur hadn't found time to strike yet.

I did a quick check of the kitchen hallway. Mary Hurst was working in there. I smelled the brownies baking.

The drawing room was empty.

Just what I needed.

I set my chronometer for a jump and surveyed the space for the best anchor location.

If I was right, this was all going to be over quickly.

I pulled out my gun and chambered a round. Didn't hurt to be cautious.

"Hey, Waldo. What's your opinion on the safest jump location in this room to get back to tomorrow night?"

"Assuming no one in the room has moved? I'd hate for you to fuze yourself into someone and die."

"That'd probably ruin my night too."

"No one was standing near the fireplace when you departed. You could use the mantle."

"My coordinates look good?"

"Precise as always."

"How do you feel about catching some bad guys?"

"I'd say, it's about time."

I set the timer on my chronometer and placed my hand on the mantle. As the seconds counted down I aimed my pistol in the direction I knew Leo would be standing.

And here we go.

I jumped.

CHAPTER 31

The room was as I'd left it.

Precisely as I'd left it, in fact, since my earlier self had just jumped away a matter of seconds ago.

Leo saw me first and swore.

"Don't try it!" I said and elevated my pistol.

He had a hand on his gun but froze.

Roman raised both of his hands. He watched me cautiously.

Ainsley let out a muffled shriek from the floor near the bar. She was still tied up near Osborne. He hadn't moved.

Mary Hurst finally wore an expression of surprise. Seeing a person walk through a time gate was one thing, but seeing them reappear out of thin air was another. I was glad to see her capable of a little awe.

"Leo, why don't you untie Miss Parker for me. But put your gun on the bar first."

He looked to his boss.

Roman nodded. "I see you've reacquired your chronometer," he said. "What does that imply about the health of our intrepid Inspector Fallgrave?"

"The health and whereabouts of the good inspector remain a mystery," I said. "As it seems he was never on this island." I pulled the false mustache from my pocket and tossed it to the coffee table.

Roman followed the motion with only vague interest.

"But I suspect you knew that already."

Leo got the cords off Ainsley's wrists and ankles and she scrambled to her feet. She pulled the gag from her mouth as she ran to me. "Oh, thank God. I knew you'd come back."

She wrapped her arms around me and pressed her face to my chest, but I didn't take my eyes off Roman.

"The question I have, is how much you knew," I continued. "Certainly enough to conspire with Weintraub to smuggle something from the past."

"That's where you're wrong," Roman said. "I didn't organize any of this. But I *was* made a promise. I provided my services for a percentage of the recovered value. It's all in writing. Would you like to see the contract?"

"No. I'm sure you've got plausible deniability. Weintraub didn't need to tell you the whole score. And he didn't want the rest of this group knowing either."

Agent Osborne groaned from the floor. Looked like he was coming around.

Just in time.

"We should help him," Ainsley said. She scurried back across the room and bent to untie Osborne.

"Not just yet."

She looked up in confusion. "Why?"

"Because I have a few questions for him."

Osborne blinked himself awake and Leo pulled him upright. He looked to Ainsley first, then around the room, his gaze finally landing on me.

"What the hell is going on here?"

"Leo thought you could do with a siesta."

Osborne scowled. "Where's . . . Constantine?"

"Same thing I wanted to ask you, since the man you came here with sure wasn't him."

Osborne finally noticed the false mustache lying on the coffee table. What little color was in his face seemed to drain away.

"You had me fooled for a while," I said. "Especially with you selling him as the real deal." I lowered my gun. "I may not know all there is to know about the way Time Crimes solves cases, but I'm pretty sure they don't knowingly send imposters. The fact that you came here with a man posing as your old partner tells me something important. It means you didn't come from Time Crimes. My guess is they have no idea you're here."

Osborne clenched his jaw and wrestled with his bonds. But he was stuck and he knew it.

"It was a nice con. Weintraub needed someone to help him sell it, no doubt. He even got a couple people involved to serve as patsies." I gestured to Roman and Leo. "Known mobster and his bodyguard. What was supposed to happen? They get involved just enough to take the fall? They kill me? I can see how any of those scenarios would have played out fine for Weintraub. As long as he had you to mop up."

"You think you're smart, huh?" Osborne said. "We'll see how far it gets you."

"It's fine. Play it tough. Once Time Crimes takes a look at Winston's killing, all the evidence is going to point to the only person I hadn't accounted for at the time. You."

"You've got no proof of any of this."

"Not yet. And Weintraub is dead, so you only have one other person to worry about spilling her guts. Isn't that right, Ainsley?"

Ainsley Parker stood rigid, with her expression frozen somewhere between shock and panic.

"Because if Osborne and Fallgrave didn't come from Time Crimes, it's because you never *called* Time Crimes. You played your part well, though. The scream in the fog, pretending you saw the shooting of Logan Tyler. Then insisting we call for help. I have to admit I never suspected you weren't really talking to TCID. And Osborne and Weintraub needed someone reliable on the inside before they arrived, didn't they? Someone who would keep an eye on things. On me?"

"I don't know what you're talking about," she said. "Don't you know I was with you the whole time?"

"Of course you were. What better way to keep tabs on my activity and report it to Weintraub. But the damsel in distress act is harder to pull off than it used to be. You think I can't tell when a woman has more brains than she's letting on?"

Her expression changed and her voice with it. "Weintraub lied to me about how far he was going to take this. Winston was never supposed to get hurt."

"The guy impersonating the cops was supposed to be trustworthy? That going to be your defense when they charge you as an accessory to Winston's murder?"

Ainsley shook her head. "I didn't murder anyone."

"Won't matter when they find out that your boyfriend here did." I looked to Osborne. "Figured no one would suspect a Time Crimes agent, right? But you were the only one besides me that knew Winston was figuring out your secret shipment coming in with the coordinates from the Warsaw Pendulum. Couldn't have him spreading that around. So Weintraub had you take him out."

Osborne just glared at me.

"And you think I didn't notice the way you looked at me and Ainsley? You're not the first jealous boyfriend I've met."

Ainsley looked to Osborne and back to me. "I swear I didn't know anything about him killing Winston. It wasn't part of the plan. And he and I weren't even that serious. We only met through Weintraub."

"Shut up!" Osborne shouted. "We can still fix this."

"No. No," I said. "This is your chance to save yourself, Ainsley. You've been playing all sides of this thing from the start. Which side are you going to choose now?"

She looked around the room. Zigzag had narrowed her eyes. Amadeus was likewise giving her a murderous glare.

But Ainsley's expression hardened too.

That's when she lunged for Leo's gun on the bar. She snatched it up and waved it around the room before pointing in my direction.

I sighed. "That was your chance."

"No. *This* is my chance," she said, readjusting her grip on the gun. Damned thing looked heavy as hell. She shouted at Zigzag. "You. Untie him."

"Fuck off," Zigzag replied.

Ainsley scowled at her, but didn't squeeze the trigger.

Roman's hand was easing under his jacket. I knew he had a gun somewhere. He looked at me. I shook my head and held up a finger.

"Think this out, Ainsley."

She swung around and pointed the gun in my direction again.

"If you can prove to a jury you didn't know Winston was going to be killed, you might not be in for any murder charges at all. You're in the risk assessment business. You're smart. You want to go down for a murder you didn't commit?"

"I'm not an idiot. They'll still tie me to killing Logan Tyler."

"How are they going to do that?"

All eyes in the room went to the doorway where Logan Tyler stood with a gun pointed at Ainsley.

Logan smiled. "Hard to do with me still alive."

Ainsley's mouth fell open. This time with genuine surprise. Her arms finally gave out and she lowered the Desert Eagle. She took another long look at Logan, then gave a defeated groan and turned toward Leo. "Seriously. How do you even shoot this damned thing?"

"Probably would have knocked your own ass out trying," he said and took the gun from her. "Honestly, it hurts my hand when I shoot it too. But you weren't in any danger. The safety was on."

Her shoulders fell. "Figures." Ainsley shuffled to the couch and slumped into the corner of the cushions. A wise choice.

I holstered my pistol. "Mary, do you have a key to Ms. Parker's room?"

Mary Hurst rose from her chair and nodded. "I can find one."

"If you search her room, I suspect we'll find the missing parts to the tachyon pulse transmitter. I think it's time we called the real cops."

CHAPTER 32

Roman Amadeus and Leo DeRossi didn't feel like sticking around till TCID showed up.

Couldn't say I blamed them. There were going to be a lot of questions.

Time Crimes agents would likely catch up with them eventually, but by then there would be a lot of confusion to sort through. Roman could force TCID to prove it wasn't some alternate version of him who attended this gathering, or employ any number of stalling tactics to hamper their investigation. It wasn't his first time playing this game, so he wouldn't lose easily.

I could have tried to hold them at gunpoint, maybe even have a shootout over it, but I didn't have that kind of investment. For all I knew, Roman was telling the truth, and Weintraub had scammed him too. I had my doubts but I was short on proof. So they walked.

Roman did make a point of speaking to me before stepping through the time gate.

"Why is it that every time I've run into you, it costs me a lot of money? I hope you don't intend to make that a trend."

"I'm nothing if not consistent," I said.

"We'll meet again, Greyson."

I'm sure he meant it to sound ominous, but I was tired. I wasn't in a mood to worry.

Zigzag didn't wait for the cops either. She reactivated the time gate as soon as Amadeus and Leo were gone. I watched.

"For what it's worth. I'm glad you didn't end up dead," she said.

"Out of everyone here, you were the only one who knew I shot Weintraub from the beginning. But you didn't out me."

"Always figured you were one kind of guy, but you had me wondering."

"I appreciate you giving me the benefit of the doubt."

She adjusted her grip on her bag. "Nobody likes to be told what bad things they might be capable of. Better if it comes as a surprise."

"What about the good things they're capable of?"

She shook her head. "Maybe for you. I'm not one of your good people. I know that."

"Better than you give yourself credit for."

She stepped toward the gate but turned around at the last second. "Just for the record. I looked at that data drive. Amadeus might not have incriminated himself with the Warsaw contraband, but he knew it existed. And judging by the contents of that drive, he's got a lot of bigger things planned."

"You didn't happen to make a copy for me, did you?"

She smirked, but backed slowly into the light of the time gate. "See you around, Travers."

The real Time Crimes agents came in force. Over a dozen of them. There was a lot of searching and questioning and gun pointing in various rooms of the lodge. Eventually the scene calmed down enough to have a conversation.

The chief investigator was named Rawlins and we got along all right. But it wasn't until another hour had passed and Agent Stella York showed up that I finally relaxed. She was out of uniform when she arrived, with the exception of her badge and gun. She was wearing her preferred bomber jacket though and it seemed to fit the climate. She consulted with Rawlins for a while before getting around to me.

I waited out on the porch and took in the view. The rain had finally stopped. Now it was just foggy again.

"This what you do on your days off?" I asked as Stella finally made her way over.

"Who ever said I get days off?" She gestured toward the group of agents inside going over evidence. "Rawlins gave me a heads up when the call came in that it was you. They know I've got a history of interest in Amadeus and the way you two collide."

"They tell you about the bodies?"

"Yeah. Apparently you need one moved?"

"Unless we want a paradox. I told your guy where it was and when. Just needs to be gone by this morning when I show up to look for it."

"Rawlins is good," she said. "They'll be careful."

"Bit of a mess to clean up."

"You okay?" She studied me. "Shooting a man is no small thing."

"I'm all right. Had to be done."

"Logan Tyler backed up your story. Sounds like it was a good shoot. Investigation will verify your self-defense claim. Turns out we had a file on Weintraub and didn't even know it. Guy's been running cons a long time. At least seven aliases that we know of. He once impersonated a senator for a week. He was good, but I think this time he took too big of a swing."

"They talk to the girl?"

"Parker? Yeah. Sounds like she's ready to spill anything we need. Should make the prosecution's life easy."

"She say how she got mixed up in this?"

"The deal went through her to be financed by the ACC. I'm guessing Weintraub saw her potential as an asset. Hard to say how long he and Osborne were planning this together, but I imagine we'll find out."

"Ainsley's more clever than she lets on, but she sails whichever way the wind's blowing."

"She try to sail your way for a while?"

I shrugged. "No accounting for taste."

"She'll no doubt work a deal for herself."

I nodded. "You going to fill me in on Osborne?"

Stella leaned on the porch railing next to me. "Word from on high is that he's been dirty for a while, they've just been building a case. This will be the nail in his coffin."

"And the real Fallgrave?"

"Retired. Has been for years. Lives in some remote timestream now. A writing cabin in the woods or something. Osborne coasted on their rep for a while, but everyone knew who the star was. Maybe he thought this situation would bring him back into the spotlight."

"What was his stake in this? You think he intended to frame Amadeus?"

"Collar like that certainly would have gotten the heat off him for a while. Probably could have ridden that glory all the way to retirement. But you and I both know Amadeus won't go down that easily."

"Was Osborne on duty here?"

"Leave of absence."

I nodded. "Explains why he didn't have a company-issued time traveling device. I should have been onto him earlier because of that."

"Don't blame yourself for missing it. Who suspects the time cops?"

I slid my hands into my coat pocket. I was starting to like this coat. Might need to keep it.

"If you're all right, I'm going to go help Rawlins for a bit," Stella said. "Getting this scene processed is going to take some work."

"Thanks for coming by."

She patted me on the shoulder and headed back inside.

I stood there staring out at the fog for a while.

Eventually I heard a click.

I turned to find Mary Hurst lowering her camera.

"Good background lighting."

I exhaled. Felt like I'd been holding my breath this whole trip. Mary checked the image.

I lifted my chin toward the camera. "Mind if I get a copy?"

She shrugged. "Sure. Time travelers use email?"

"We do."

She scrolled across the digital display. "Made quite the album this trip. Usually it's all birds."

"You doing okay? This must be a lot to take in."

"I'll have some time to think about it. Figure it will be quiet for a bit till the boat arrives."

I'd forgotten she had another week on this island.

"What do you do the rest of the year? Who's Mary Hurst when she's not an Attu wildlife photographer and birding lodge hostess?"

"Nobody special. This is the real me out here. Rest of the time is just me trying to get somewhere like this."

"Hope you enjoy the rest of your stay then."

"Oh, I will. Once all the murderers are gone."

I chuckled and left her on the porch to enjoy the quiet.

Logan Tyler was in one of the guest rooms with a TCID

agent taking scans of the Warsaw Pendulum.

She turned to me as I walked in. "Sounds like they are going to let you have it once they're done here."

"We certainly worked hard enough for it."

The agent with the scanner addressed me. "We'll be in touch with Mrs. Rosen regarding the recovery phase. If there is a suspicion of illegal contraband being moved through time, we have to investigate."

"I'd expect nothing less."

He waved toward the bed where the pendulum was laid out. "It's all yours then." He left the room.

Logan still had dirt on her clothes from the crawlspace, but looked otherwise no worse for wear.

"Sorry you had such a long day."

"All part of the job," she said. "The brownies and champagne cheered me up considerably."

"You got some reading in too?"

"Couldn't resist looking up this Fallgrave guy when I saw his name in the library. Sounds like he has a good methodology."

"If he'd been here for real, it probably would have saved us a lot of trouble."

"I don't know," she said. "I'm glad you were here instead. You were right about what you told Weintraub. Sometimes you have to trust your gut."

"I was keeping a promise," I said.

"To someone smart, no doubt." She buttoned her coat. "Well, I guess my job is done here."

"Maybe I'll see you around."

"Because it's such a small multiverse?" she laughed.

"Seems like it some days."

She grinned and put her hand out. "Thanks for saving my life, Greyson Travers."

I shook her hand. "Any time."

CHAPTER 33

Rachel Rosen held the Warsaw Pendulum across her lap, running a finger over the Star of David engraved at the end. The door to the grandfather clock sat open behind her desk.

"You have everything you need?" I asked.

She took off her glasses and appraised me. There was a tear in her eye. She wiped it away quickly. "Indeed I do. Though the Temporal Crimes Investigation Division has laid claim to the shipment for the time being."

"Weintraub had a lot riding on it."

"It's all right. I have a large team of absurdly priced lawyers. The Warsaw resistance cache will be back in the proper hands in short order."

"Good to know that's settled. And our business is done?"

She folded her hands over the pendulum. "It would seem so. You've been a man of your word. I'll keep my end of the bargain as well. Consider yours and Miss Archer's financial obligations met."

I nodded.

"It's regrettable that our relationship started the way it did. I trust there are no hard feelings?"

"Difficult to hold you responsible when it turns out I had a lot to do with the circumstances."

She cupped her chin with a thumb and forefinger. "I know we didn't discuss any further payment for your services, so it's a bit late for that now. But I invite you to stay on at the Rose 'n Bridge as long as you like. Whenever you need a place there, it's yours."

"That's generous. Thank you."

"No. Thank you, Mr. Travers. You've brought a piece of my family's history home to rest. And I'm grateful."

I rose from my chair. "I'll be going."

Rosen moved a hand to the conference controls. "Shalom, Mr. Travers. Till we meet again."

The room blinked back to the way it had looked before. Just old bookshelves and armchairs.

I walked back into the hall and wended my way to the tavern end of the inn.

The pub was still quiet. Heavens and Sol were chatting at the bar near my usual seat.

Heavens smiled at me as I walked in. She gestured to the pile of belongings I'd left on the bar.

"You starting a scrapbooking project?"

I slid onto the barstool next to Sol and removed the new picture frame from the shopping bag. "Nothing that sentimental." I next pulled out the pack of Sharpie markers and the hard photo envelope. Inside I had the copy of the photo Mary Hurst had taken of me outside the lodge on Attu.

Heavens reached into the bag and pulled out the original photo I'd received from Rosen, now battered from travel. She compared the photos. "So it was *you* who mailed her the picture to begin with?"

"Apparently. Found this frame in a shop down the road this

morning. But I don't recognize the handwriting on the back of the photo. It's not mine."

She slid the original photo out of the frame and looked at the coordinates printed on the back. "Not mine either." She showed it to Sol.

"Oh shit," Sol muttered.

"That's your handwriting?" I asked.

"Why are you dragging me into your paradoxical ontological nonsense?"

"Technically, if you help, we're *preventing* an ontological paradox."

"Just give me the damn markers." She swiped the pack of Sharpies from my hand.

Heavens read off the coordinates from the back of the original while Sol wrote on my new photo that would become the original.

In a few minutes we had the photo created and ready to mail to Rosen in the past. I'd need to jump back a week or two to find a post office but it would work out. Apparently it already had.

Heavens picked up the wrinkled version I'd originally received. "What are you going to do with this one?"

"Throw it out, probably."

"What? No. It's a good photo. Artistic."

"At least that angle doesn't show my black eye."

"I thought that was just the way you looked all the time," Sol said.

"Ha. Ha."

"I'm putting it up behind the bar," Heavens said, sliding the photo back into its frame and looking around at the shelves. She tried it out near a cluster of other knick knacks, then pulled a signed baseball from Babe Ruth off the shelf and tossed it aside. She stuck my photo there instead.

"Hey," I muttered, watching the ball go rolling away down

the bar. "You even know who that was?"

"Yeah. The big guy. Whatshisface. He was a good tipper, but I don't know why he gave me that ball."

I sighed.

Sol climbed off her stool. "Well, this has been fun, but I have work to do." She handed me the Sharpie she'd used. "Still kinda sad you didn't die and leave us your car, but I guess it's good to have you back or whatever."

"When I get it fixed, I'll take you for a ride."

"Ride? Shit, I want to drive."

"We can probably work that out."

She clapped her hands together. "Okay, now I'm actually glad you're back." She threw a fist bump out to Heavens. "Peace, baby. I'll catch you later."

Heavens bumped her fist and smiled. "Next batch of tourists, here we come."

When Sol was gone, Heavens turned her attention back to me. "With your car broken, does that mean you have to stick around for a while to wait for the part?"

"Actually, Rosen said I have a room here as long as I want. Figured I might hang around a bit and see what kind of trouble I can get into."

Heavens grinned. "Kinda hoped you'd say that." She reached under the bar and pulled up a box. "'Cause I got you a present."

The box looked heavy.

"No way. Is that what I think it is?"

"It's your flux capacitor thingy. Waldo sent me the part number."

"Temporal ground analyzer," I muttered. "I can't believe you got it in already."

"Thought you might need it. And I thought we might need a way to go get you next time someone is plotting your murder on some far away island."

I stared across the bar at her. "I think you might be the perfect woman."

"FYI. It was expensive. You can pay me back later."

We stared at each other for a long moment, and everything else in the room seemed to fade away. But Heavens broke eye contact.

"Hey, you never answered my question from before," I said, not wanting to waste the moment. "The boyfriend from the future rumor. Seriously. He around or not?"

Heavens shook her head. "You still haven't figured that out yet?"

"Should I have?"

"Do you *want* me to have a boyfriend in the future?"

"I mean, I wouldn't mind *being* your boyfriend in the future." I let the words hang in the air.

Finally, she shrugged. "Maybe you will be." She poured me a beer.

My heart was racing. "Hang on. You're saying that all this time the rumors that you have a boyfriend from the future meant that you have a boyfriend who might just be me *in the future?*"

"Not yet." She slid me the beer.

"What do you mean, not yet?

"It's still in the future. You're not ready." She pointed to the beer. "That's to drown your sorrows while you wait."

She wiped off her hands on a rag and tossed it in the laundry bin.

I sat there with my mouth open.

She gave me another wink, and walked away through the doors to the kitchen.

I stared after her. Eventually my mouth started functioning again.

"Wait. What's your definition of 'the future?'"

I didn't get a response.

Holy hell.

I rested my elbows on the bar and picked up the beer. I studied the back of the bar. The picture of Attu on the shelf did look pretty good up there. And it seemed I had a new prospect.

I smiled and sipped the beer.

Some futures were worth the wait.

Thanks for reading! The adventures of Greyson Travers will continue. Want to be sure to never miss a release? Let your future self know by subscribing at NathanVanCoops.com

You can start a free time travel story now. Read on for a sneak preview of Clockwise and Gone.

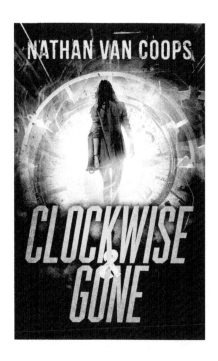

Clockwise & Gone

Chapter 1

"To your promotion," Dom said, raising the glass of champagne. "New head of Gammatech's Safety Division."

Emily reached for her nearly-empty glass and held it aloft gently. "Thanks to you."

"I had hardly anything to do with it." Dom snatched the bottle from the bucket of ice and quickly topped off her champagne flute. "Management at Gammatech just knows a winner when they see one." He grinned and clinked his glass against hers. "You earned it."

Emily smiled and took a sip. She certainly had done everything in her power to prove herself at the energy company but that hadn't stopped the rumors and muttering behind her back—the whispers that she was only where she was because she had slept her way to the top. Dom laughed off the idea that anyone would doubt her resume, but no one had ever said anything to him directly. He was Dominic Del Toro, son of the owner of the company. He was immune.

Emily was not.

She had no doubt that there would be sideways glances on Monday when she was back at the office, but she was determined to enjoy the champagne anyway. She took another sip and took in the expansive view of the illuminated city skyline. She would enjoy tonight. Monday's problems could wait.

The server's reflection in the glass made her turn her gaze back to the bustling restaurant.

"Can I interest you in any dessert this evening?" He cleared away her plate and handed it off to a passing busboy.

"I actually hoped we could have the special tonight, Felipe. The one I called ahead about?" Dom said.

"Of course, sir." Felipe smiled. "I'll get that for you right away."

"Call-ahead special?" Emily asked. "Wow. Courtside seats at the game, now specialty desserts— you really did go all out tonight."

"Well, not quite yet," Dom said. He slid out of his seat and reached into his pocket as he stood. "There was one more thing I was hoping to discuss. One question that wasn't in your interview from the board yesterday."

Emily stared at the small black box in his hand. He was getting on one knee. Oh wow, this was happening now?

"Emily Marie Davis, from the first time I saw you, I was completely and utterly in love with you. Even all the way back at uni when you wouldn't give me the time of day." Dom smiled at her. "I would do absolutely anything to keep you in my life forever. Would you do me the honor of marrying me?"

Emily stared at the sparkling diamond as he opened the box, and realized her hand was shaking when some champagne sloshed onto the table. She hastily set the glass down.

"Oh my God. I can't believe you are doing this." Marriage. This was really happening.

He grinned up at her. "So, what do you say? Would you like to be Mrs. Del Toro?"

Emily looked into his eager eyes and slid out of her chair. Her breath seemed caught inside her, but finally she got the words out. "Yes, of course. Yes."

He stood to wrap his arms around her and she pressed her lips to his. Over the thrumming of her heartbeat in her ears, she registered the clapping and cheering of the other diners in the restaurant. But just barely. They may as well have been in another world.

The elevator ride to the street was a blur. She didn't even remember leaving the restaurant. There had been a dessert. A cake? She vaguely recalled that much. Another bottle of champagne had been opened too. That was still with them. Dom carried the half empty bottle with him to the car. As his vehicle pulled to the curb they climbed into the back laughing.

"Home, Avery," Dom managed, before Emily tackled him and started planting kisses all over his face.

"Proceeding to Regency Tower." The car's automated response system flashed the destination on a screen and engaged its drive motor.

Emily stopped kissing Dom long enough to admire the ring on her finger again. He'd really outdone himself this time.

"You like it?" Dom studied her with eager eyes.

"I love it. It's beautiful."

"Still doesn't compare to you," Dom replied.

As Emily reached for him again, the car's speaker came on and the voice of Dom's life management system, Avery, spoke. "A call coming in for you, sir. Inspector Walsh from subsection Delta."

"I'm a little busy right now," Dom replied between Emily's smothering kisses.

"He's all mine tonight, Avery," Emily said.

"The call is marked urgent," Avery replied. "How would you like me to respond?"

"Inspectors always think everything is urgent," Dom said. "Tell him I'll call him back."

"Yes, sir," Avery replied.

The car arrived at Regency Tower entirely too quickly as far as Emily was concerned. She had barely gotten Dom's tie off him, let alone anything else. He was altogether too buttoned up for her taste.

They were engaged. She had a fiance. It had seemed like a made-up word till now.

She let it roll around her mind as she carried her shoes and let Dom lead her toward the elevator. Her head was decidedly fuzzy from the champagne, but something about the ring on her finger was making him irresistible tonight. She entwined her fingers through his and leaned her head onto his shoulder in the elevator. He was wearing the cologne she'd gotten him for Christmas. She took a deep breath. Yes. This was going to be a good night.

Dom wasn't the most physically attractive man she had ever dated. If you had asked her yesterday she might even have said he wasn't in the top five. He lacked the height and athleticism she usually looked for. She had always dated ball players in college. Dom's physique was far better suited for a golf course than a basketball court. His jump shot was atrocious. He worked out when he could, but as heir to the Gammatech empire, he spent far more time in board meetings than at the gym. Add in the receding hairline, and Dom might even be considered homely by some. But what he lacked in looks he had more than made up for in devotion.

Ever since she moved back to the city, he'd been pursuing her. No. Longer than that. She could remember him trying to walk her home from parties in college, back before he'd lost his glasses. He'd always had style, and women interested in his money certainly fawned over him, but he used to show up to her games in a suit and tie. Not at all what she was looking for then. He'd even visited her in the hospital the night she tore her ACL and ended her dreams of going pro. Despite his continued attention, she'd barely given him a second glance. During the years since college she rarely thought of him at all unless it was at

Christmas or her birthday. He always remembered to send a card. Real mail. Hardly anyone did that anymore.

Those were the little things that added up in the end.

When she finished with her energy contracts abroad and decided to search for a job back in the states, it was Dom that had contacted her immediately. He said he'd seen her resume and thought she'd be a wonderful fit at Gammatech. A management track with a salary that made competitor's offers look laughable. How could she say no?

The doors dinged open at the penthouse. His penthouse. Would they live here after they were married? The thought gave her pause. This was all happening so fast.

"Avery, please set lights to level 2," Dom said as they entered.

The normally bright lighting dimmed to a soft glow.

"Are you feeling okay?" Dom asked, smiling at her. Emily realized she was still latched to his arm and slowly unwrapped herself.

"Yes. But I think I need more champagne. You'll go find us some?"

Dom brushed a strand of her hair behind her ear. "I'm already as elated as I've ever been. More booze won't help."

Emily grabbed his hand and kissed his fingers. "Yes, but I need a minute to get sexy for you."

"You're already sexy," Dom grinned.

"Champagne," Emily commanded, pointing toward the kitchen. "Your fiancee says she needs champagne!"

He let go of her fingers and bowed, then turned toward the kitchen.

She did not need more champagne.

Her head was already swimming, but she was going to do this right. She pushed through the door to his bedroom and dropped her shoes near the closet doors. She should have planned ahead better. If she had known this was coming she would have tried to stash something here to wear. Something other than the yoga pants and old sweatshirt she kept stuffed in the bottom drawer of his dresser for nights she slept over. That wasn't going to cut it tonight.

She considered just stripping bare on the bed and waiting, but shook off the thought. She was feeling far too full from dinner to be up for that. She would opt for one of his button-down shirts. It wasn't lingerie, but he'd still like it. Can't beat the classics.

A cork popped from somewhere in the vicinity of the living room.

She ditched her dress on the floor and walked to the bathroom mirror to determine the appropriate amount of buttons to employ on the shirt. Once there she took a look at the state of her wavy chestnut hair and frowned. She was trying to get it back into some semblance of a style when Avery chimed from the other room.

"Call from Inspector Danvers, marked as urgent."

"Danvers?" Dom asked. "From Sector Echo?"

"Yes. There are also three other inspectors on the line. They've requested you join a community call. Shall I engage a video conference?"

"No!" Emily shouted from the bathroom. "He's busy."

"No video," Dom said as he walked into the bedroom.

"Hey, I'm not ready for you yet," Emily said. "You go there." She pointed him toward the bed.

"I might need to take this call," Dom said. "It sounds important."

"It's Saturday night. We just got engaged. Can't it wait?"

"I'm just going to see what's going on. Maybe it's nothing."

Avery chimed in. "Mr. Del Toro Senior has also joined the call but is requesting a private conversation."

Dom squeezed Emily's hand, then walked back into the other room.

Emily frowned and slumped onto the bed.

"Avery?"

"Yes, Miss Davis?"

"We're going to need to talk about his priorities . . ."

"I would be happy to provide any service Dom requires," Avery replied.

"I'll bet you would," Emily muttered.

She propelled herself off the bed and only wavered momentarily before pushing her way out the door to the living room.

Dom had his jacket back on and was attempting to retie his tie.

"You're leaving?" Emily said. "Where are you going?"

"I need to get down to the plant and check on things. This new shipment of control rods I ordered for the reactor is giving us some strange indications. The inspectors called a meeting. I guess it's pretty serious."

"Is everyone at the plant okay?"

"Yeah, absolutely. Just stay here. I'll be back as soon as I can." He finished the tie, then patted his jacket pockets, doing an inventory, before stepping over and kissing her. "Don't go anywhere."

"Fine," Emily said, pouting her lower lip, but adjusting his collar to better cover the tie.

He kissed her one more time, then slipped out the door. "Be back soon."

Emily stood staring at the closed door for a few seconds, then turned slowly on her heel to check her other options. The newly opened bottle of champagne was still sitting on the counter. She slouched over to it and snatched one of the glasses up before trudging back to the bedroom.

"Looks like it's just the two of us, Avery."

"Would you like to view entertainment options, Miss Davis?

Perhaps the highlights from the afternoon's games?"

"Not tonight. I think I just want a bath. Will you fill the tub?"

"Bathtub will be filled in approximately eleven minutes. Would you like to choose a scent for your bath oils?"

"What does Dom use?"

"Mr. Del Toro prefers lavender and tea tree."

"Interesting. I'll try that." Emily took a sip of champagne. "And some music please." The penthouse filled with soothing instrumental piano music. "Something from this century," Emily said.

She was still bickering with Avery about the music choices when she heard the elevator ding in the hall. A moment later, footsteps sounded in the kitchen.

She opened the bedroom door and looked back out. "Dom?"

Dom had his back to her, rooting through a drawer in the kitchen, but turned around at the sound of her voice.

"That was fast," Emily said. "False alarm?"

He wasn't wearing a tie anymore. He looked . . . tired. Like the few minutes he'd been gone had aged him.

"Hello, Emily," Dom said. He stared at her, looking her up and down. "You look . . . well."

Well? She was half-naked in his shirt wearing a brand new engagement ring and 'well' was the best compliment he could muster?

"What happened?" she said aloud.

"We need to go," Dom replied. He strode across the room and grabbed her by the wrist.

"What? Go where?"

But he was already pulling her across the room toward the elevator.

"Dom, I can't go anywhere. I'm not dressed and it's late. I thought we were staying in. Ow. You're hurting me."

Dom's grip on her wrist was like a vice. He dragged her into the foyer. The elevator doors opened and he spun her inside.

"I don't have my shoes," Emily objected.

"You don't need them."

"Where are we going?"

He didn't reply. He was preoccupied with checking his phone. He studied the time, then shoved the phone back in his pocket. Emily stared at him but he seemed intent on ignoring her.

His face was stubbled. Hadn't he been clean shaven earlier tonight? Emily studied the shadow on his chin with confusion. How much champagne had she drunk? Things were getting strange.

The elevator reached the garage level and Dom hauled her forward across the oil-stained concrete to a waiting car. It wasn't his car, but Dom flung the door open without a moment's hesitation. "Come on. Get in."

"I want your jacket."

"What?"

"Give me your jacket. You're hauling me off to somewhere you won't explain. I'm not going in just your shirt."

"Why does it matter?" Dom asked. "We won't be seeing anyone."

Emily held out her hand for the jacket.

Dom sighed and took it off, then tossed it to her. He pushed her toward the car. Come on. We've got to go."

Emily climbed into the rear-facing bench seat and slipped her arms into the jacket. She wrapped it around herself and tucked her dirty feet up underneath her.

"Why on earth can't we just stay in the penthouse? What's the big hurry?"

Dom was glancing at his phone again. "You'll know soon enough. Avery, take us to Section Kilo."

"The research division?" Emily asked. Gammatech had what

seemed like a thousand departments on a dozen campuses around the city, but she'd made a point of learning them all.

"Here. I need you to drink this." Dom held out a glass bottle of bright blue liquid. "It'll help you sober up."

"Then you drink it," Emily replied. "You're the one acting like a crazy person."

Dom shrugged, unscrewed the cap on the bottle, and took a swig. Then he held it out to her again.

Emily glared at him, but then took the bottle. Her head was beginning to throb. Hydration wasn't a bad idea. She took a sip and let the blue liquid course down her throat. It tasted like . . . What was it? Something she'd never felt. Like liquid lightning. Her throat tingled with it.

She considered Dom seated across from her. He was simply staring out the window. She sniffed and wrinkled her nose, then tried to locate the scent she was smelling. It was coming from his jacket. She lifted the collar and held it to her nose. Cologne. But one she'd never smelled before. When would he have had time to get more cologne? The bathtub hadn't even filled in the time he was gone.

She looked at her fiance across the back of the car. His expression was hard to read in the shadowy interior.

He *had* been clean shaven tonight. All those kisses.

"Dom?" she tried softly this time. "What's going on?"

When he looked at her, his eyes were serious. "You'll just have to trust me."

"But why can't you tell me what's happening? I'm getting frightened. You're freaking me out."

"Emily." He leaned forward and rested a hand on her knee. "In all the time you've known me, has there ever been anything I've done that wasn't in the interest of keeping you with me? Of keeping you safe?"

"No. Never."

"Then believe me when I tell you now. There is nothing I wouldn't do to keep you from harm."

"Are we in danger?" Emily asked.

Dom looked back out the window as the vehicle slowed. "Not for much longer. Drink the rest of that, then come on. We're here."

Chapter 2

The concrete sidewalk leading to the research facility was cold on Emily's bare feet. She shivered a little and wrapped Dom's jacket around herself a little tighter. A security guard at the entrance tipped his hat to Dom.

"Good to see you again, sir. Twice in one night." He smiled and opened the door for them.

The doorway traded cold concrete for cold epoxy flooring that was slick beneath her feet.

Dom didn't slow his pace at all as he guided her through several hallways to what must have been the back of the building. He finally stopped at a doorway that had been chained shut and padlocked. Dom entered a combination and unlocked it, then pulled the entire chain free. Emily noticed that the combination had been her birthday, 4-9-20. Dom took a glance down the hallway they came from, then pulled the door open. "Okay. Here we go."

Emily wasn't sure what she expected, but the room they walked into wasn't it. It looked like an oversized storage closet. Dusty metal racks lined the walls, home for a few outdated computers and forgotten hard drives. There was a window on the far end of the room but the opaque glass squares only let in the faintest glow from the streetlight. Dom flipped the switch and illuminated the room with harsh fluorescent light.

He ran the chain through the door handles again and refastened the lock.

"About time," someone said. "I thought you said you'd be quick."

Emily located the speaker sitting in a folding chair in the corner. He rocked forward and stood, shaking out the length of his overcoat and stomping his feet. He was skinny, dressed in all black, and smoking an electronic cigarette. She hadn't seen one of those in years.

"Why are you just lurking here in the dark?" Dom said. "It's creepy."

"You wanted me to stay here. I stayed. You didn't say you needed me awake."

Dom turned toward Emily. "This is a new acquaintance of mine. What did you say your name was again?"

"Axle."

"Well, Axle, did you at least prepare things for me like I asked you to?"

"Setup's all ready. Standard stuff." He pointed to a rolling office chair and a contraption against the wall that looked like some kind of door frame.

"Dom, what's going on?" Emily said. "You really need to tell me what we're doing here. Who is this guy?"

"We're getting away for a little," Dom said. "I've got somewhere where we can go to get things sorted out. I've got a way to keep you safe."

Emily noticed that Axle was eyeing her bare legs and tried to tug the edge of Dom's jacket a little lower.

"You don't mind me saying so, mack, you got a fine looking lady here. Lots going for you. You sure you don't want to just forget this plan and go off and enjoy her somewhere? I'm thinking I would."

"Shut your damn mouth," Dom growled at him. "I didn't pay you for your suggestions. I paid you to do your job. Just get things ready. We're wasting time."

Axle held up his hands. "Whatever you say, mack. You're the boss." He stepped over to the doorframe erected by the wall and started fiddling with a control panel attached to the side. A number of heavy-duty cables were running across the floor and were directly wired into the breaker box on the wall.

"Emily, I need to tell you something," Dom said. "I'm sorry to keep you in the dark about this but we're almost safe. There is going to be a problem at the plant. The reactor core is growing unstable. It's going to . . . It's going to do a lot of damage. But I have somewhere to take us. I can fix things. I just need you to come with me. It's all going to be okay."

"The main reactor?"

As she spoke, the door frame against the wall started buzzing. The space between the posts began to shimmer, then erupted into a field of multicolored light. The colors swirled and twisted in an eerie sort of harmony with one another. Emily found herself transfixed by their beauty.

"What is that?" she murmured.

"Our future," Dom replied. "Have a seat."

Dom wheeled a rolling office chair over and Emily sat, almost automatically, her eyes still glued to the luminescent doorway. She didn't look away until something cold closed over her wrist. She looked down to find her arm handcuffed to the chair.

"Hey, what the hell?"

"Standard procedure," Axle muttered from next to her.

"Procedure for what?" Emily demanded.

Dom shoved Axle out of the way and knelt in front of Emily.

He rested a hand on her knee, then held up another bottle of blue liquid. "I need you to drink this."

"What the hell is that stuff, Dom? And don't give me that 'sober you up' bullshit."

"It's going to help stabilize your cells," Dom replied. "The more we get into you, the safer you'll be."

Axle wheeled an IV rack over to her chair and started prepping a syringe.

"You have got to be kidding," Emily replied. She snatched the bottle from his hand and threw it across the room. "I'm not drinking anything until you explain what you're doing to me."

Dom closed his eyes for a moment, then grabbed her arm and took her hand between his. "Emily." He opened his eyes again and stared into hers. "That machine over there is going to take us somewhere new. But in order to get there, we need to treat your body with a special sort of particle. It will protect you and enable you to travel safely. But only if we get enough into you to make it work."

"Why aren't you cuffed to a chair? Why isn't he?" She looked to Axle who was now wheeling some other contraption made of hollow tubing toward them.

"We've already had our treatment," Dom replied. He kissed her hand then laid her forearm against the arm of the chair. "Now I need you to stay still." He wrapped a fabric strap quickly around her arm and fastened the Velcro.

"Hey! No. Dom!" Emily tried to jerk her arm loose but it was strapped tight. She tried moving her other arm but the metal handcuffs only rattled against the chair. "I don't want to do this. Let me go!"

"There is no other way," Dom replied. He grasped her face between his hands. "Your future depends on this."

"Dom." She stared at him with her most no-nonsense expression. "I want to go home. Let. Me. Go."

But Dom simply strapped a band around her other arm and secured it tightly to the chair as well. Axle bent down with the needle.

"Get that away from me!" she shouted.

"It's going to hurt more if you move," Axle replied. He pressed on the inside of her arm, probing for her vein.

"Don't you touch me with that—" she began, but it was too late. He already started inserting the needle. She froze. When the IV was in, he taped the tube to her arm and stood up.

She caught him staring down her shirt. She jerked against the arm of the chair but it was no use. Why hadn't she used . . . more . . . buttons . . .

She felt dizzy. Her head lolled slightly.

"What else did you put in there?" Dom asked.

"Just something to calm her down. Figured we may as well get a head start on the rest of it."

Dom frowned but didn't object. He stood, and swayed with the rest of the room as it turned. It was all getting wavy.

Emily's pulse was throbbing in her ears with the rhythm of a clock but the men seemed to be moving in slow motion. She tilted her head as Axle wheeled the tubular structure overtop of her seat. It was a sort of framework, bolted together with space in the interior for her, and with what looked to be plastic sheeting around the edges. She felt like she was in a portable shower. A bright light illuminated the sheeting. It was clear, but difficult to see through. The room had been going blurry before, but now it was even more difficult to see. Dom was just a vague shape on the other side of the curtain.

"Dom?" Her voice came out softer than she intended. She meant to yell at him but it only sounded like pleading.

"Where are you—" the air crackled with static and blue light flickered around the curtain. She saw now that it wasn't plastic, but rather some sort of conductive material ribbed with fine strands of metal. Electricity danced and tingled across her skin and seemed to burn through her veins. She cried out from the shock of it.

Moments later it was over.

The two men were muttering something on the other side of the curtain, continuing to ignore her, when a loud bang erupted near the doorway. A blinding light flashed, causing her to squint and blink, and then there were voices. The overhead lights went out. Her ears were ringing. Axle shouted. Something crashed to the floor amid a scuffle ahead of her.

"Get her loose!" a man shouted.

Someone collided with the curtain and she caught a glimpse of Axle, snarling and drawing a knife from his belt. The multicolored light emanating from the strange doorway behind her was barely enough to see anything, but she felt hands on her right arm, someone unwrapping the Velcro straps.

"Dom?"

But it wasn't Dom. A face in a black ski mask appeared in front of her. They unstrapped her other arm.

"Listen, you have to run!" It was a woman's voice.

"No! Don't touch her!" Dom shouted as he flung the tubular framework aside and grabbed for the woman in the mask. She backed away and he pursued her, fist raised.

Emily tried to rise from the chair but her left arm was still handcuffed to it. She wobbled and sat back down. What had they given her?

She was about to try again, but then Axle was there, his leering expression illuminated by the eerie flickering light. "You ain't going anywhere, honey. Except gone." He put a hand on the chair arm, and the other over her handcuffed wrist. Then he pushed her, hard, toward the multi-colored doorway. His hand ripped the IV from her arm as he shoved. "Have a nice trip!"

"No, wait!" Dom shouted.

Emily attempted to plant her feet to stop her momentum but her bare heels just slid across the slick epoxy floor. The wheels of the office chair wobbled but her trajectory was true. She rolled right into the swirl of light and color.

There was a fraction of a moment where she felt like she'd departed her body and was soaring through the cosmos.

Then the wheel of the office chair hit something and she tipped, nearly spilling out of it onto the floor. The chair teetered, then settled back onto its wheels, planting her in the seat in a room once again filled with fluorescent light. There was a medical table, some silver trays on wheels, and someone standing in front of her. She looked up to find a man in paper scrubs and latex gloves looming over her. He was wearing a paper mask and had a foot jammed against one of the chair's wheels.

"Well, what did Axle bring us today?" the man asked.

Footsteps sounded from behind her and when she spun around in the chair she found a second masked doctor on her other side. He was holding a scalpel. "Not bad looking, this time," he said. "Pity. Get her on the table. Let's open her up."

Continue this adventure for free here:

https://BookHip.com/DLSLZMV

ACKNOWLEDGMENTS

I have an incredible team that helps these books become what they are.

I'd especially like to thank the Type Pros, who are the first to ever see my work and give feedback. Every book I write is better because of you. I'd like to specifically thank: Marilyn Bourdeau, Maarja Kruusmets, Judy Eiler, Rick Bradley, Eric Lizotte, Elaine Davis, Mark Hale, Sarah Van Coops-Bush, Steve Bryant, Ginelle Blanch, Alissa Nesson, Felicia Rodriguez, Ken Robbins, Bethany Cousins, Claire Manger, and Yvonne Mitchell.

Conversations with H. Claire Taylor and her Story Alignment service at FFS.media have become an essential part of how I plot and outline my novels. Her knowledge of character and story is tremendous and I recommend her to any authors looking to write the best story they are capable of.

I'd also like to thank author Alan Lee for always being ready for a call. His listening ear and knowledge of the genre has helped guide me in the creation of Greyson and this world. His Mackenzie August series was a big part of what drew me into this genre and it's a journey I'm thrilled to be on.

The writing spots I choose around town are my favorites because they have the best people. I'd especially like to thank Hernan Nova, Casey Hengstebeck and Kimberly Porter, at Banyan Cafe, as well as Kensie Yarbrough, Dan Schmidt and Katherine Grey at Uptown Eats.

St. Pete is a far cooler place because you are in it.

The reason my life is as wonderful as it is, I owe largely to my beautiful wife Stephanie. Her support and encouragement of my writing has given me the freedom to explore more of my imagination. But it's hard to imagine a better partner to go through this adventure of life with.

And my biggest thanks is to you, my reader, for taking a chance on my stories and continuing to love these characters. If you keep reading, I'll keep writing.

If you'd like to keep in touch, my most frequent online hangout is The Tempus Fugitives Facebook group. Or connect via email at nathan@nathanvancoops.com

Till next time...

-NVC

OTHER SERIES BY NATHAN VAN COOPS

In Times Like These

The Kingdom of Engines

The Skylighter Adventures

Nathan Van Coops lives in St. Petersburg, Florida on a diet comprised mainly of tacos. When not tinkering on old airplanes, he writes heroic adventure stories that explore imaginative new worlds. He is the author of the time travel adventure series *In Times Like These*, and *Paradox PI*, as well as *The Skylighter Adventures*. His recent series, *Kingdom of Engines* explores a swashbuckling alternate history where the modern and medieval collide.

Get a free book at https://dl.bookfunnel.com/wvt1a0orfj

Cover image by Damonza

Author photo by Jennie Thunell Photography

Ebook ISBN: 978-1-950669-15-8

Paperback ISBN: 978-1-950669-16-5

Hardcover ISBN: 978-1-950669-17-2

Thanks for reading!

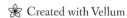 Created with Vellum

Printed in Great Britain
by Amazon

19589561R00120